DEDICATION

I dedicate this book to:

God, who is the source of all my gifts and blessings.

My daughters, Dominique and Keana, thank you for sharing your time and listening to all of my crazy stories as they poured out of my head. I celebrate your differences and encourage you to become the wonderful women of God you are meant to be.

My granddaughter Janiyah, may you remain the firecracker you are now and may that energy be poured out for the glory of God.

John and Beatrice Judkins, my wonderful parents; you have supported me in all of my endeavors whether big or small. You encouraged my gifts, offered tough love when needed, and wiped my tears when I turned to you.

To Jenine Harris, my sister from another mother, our friendship is priceless. I appreciate your husband William sharing you with me. Give my niece Jamella a big sloppy kiss from her other auntie. Thank you to Joe and Dorothy Todd, Jenine's parents, who have adopted me and my girls. I also want to thank Erica, Lisa, and Joann, Jenine's sisters, for letting me tag along.

My family members: Timothy Lee and Tony Judkins, my brothers, love you to pieces. My cousins Eleanor and Bobby Everett, Bobby and Teya Williams, Berni Greenlee, Kevin and Malisa Greenlee, Tammy Latimore—you guys have laughed at some of my zaniest moments in life. My uncle Eugene Judkins, who has weathered the storms of life and remains standing as a testimony of God's goodness, I love you.

Millie McGhee, my mentor, and founder of New Writers in Action. Your persistence, honesty, and dedication to your craft inspired me to write when I didn't feel like it. Thank you to my fellow authors Patrice Brown, Davita Carpenter, and Reggie Bishop. We all did it. I'm proud of each one of you and can't wait to read all of your books.

I appreciate the women who have looked out for me through the years—Godma Janie Mae Little, Mrs. Barbara Booker, Jackie and Tracy Jackson, Ms. Ella and her daughters Semica and Mae, Ms. Sarah Montgomery (RIP) and her family (Ms. Aretha, Sherry, Pam and Vicki), Big Anna Williams (RIP), Fredda Blackman, and my Maryland ladies: Barbara Turner, Audrey Simpson, Gwen Hammond (RIP), Robin Williams, Darlene and Tracy Booker, Michelle Penn, Denita McDaniels, Debbie Bradley, Tara Lantieri, and Vicki Mulroney.

My spiritual leaders Mike and Becky McDermott (Lifesource Church), Allan and Peggy Gorman (Harford Community Church), and Bishop Courtney and Janene McBath (Calvary Revival Ministries); thank you for your guidance, your leadership, your faithfulness to God and your congregations, and most importantly for loving your wives as Christ loved the church.

To all of my single friends both male and female, I suggest we wait on God to send the one we prayed for and watch God work. He will send us exactly who we need, the one who will love us unconditionally, and fully as God loved the church.

All of the HR staff with whom I have had the pleasure of working with over the years. We work hard to make certain everyone has what they need. We try to find creative ways to make the mission move forward, and are often the scapegoats for when it falls apart. It's usually because they don't listen to our guidance but that is beside the point. Keep in mind all characters are fictional and exist in my head. If you find something that reminds you of someone else, it's coincidental.

Most of all my readers—I hope you walk away laughing out loud, which is how I try to live my life. Be blessed.

FOREWORD

When I met this new writer, Hattye Knight, she walked into my life ready to become an author, and passionate about making her dreams come true. Her ability to write a mystery full of drama took me by surprise. It kept us all on the edge of our seats, as she shared her talent of describing elements of this story that kept you waiting for more. This is a book that will be hard to put down because it twists, twines, twirls, loops, and it interweaves you into the characters with a fascinating hook that makes this work an exciting read.

The journey with this work, *Against Company Policy*, was very interesting. The writer came in with nothing on paper, but an idea of a story, and a passion to make it happen, which was a challenge. "She was on fire, and this work took on wings and started to fly."

Mentoring, reviewing, and watching Hattye's work take wings and fly helped me consider taking on other new writers in the future. I need to say, "I am so inspired by her tenacity and pride in staying the course because she turned out a great work."

Against Company Policy, will keep you on the edge of your seat and give other new writers encouragement to go forward and be inspired.

Ms. Millie L. McGhee, Author, *Drifted Back In Time*

PROLOGUE

Think back to your first full-time job. Do you remember anything about the process? Most applicants don't give the Human Resources staff a second thought after the rejection letter. Some view them as a necessary evil to get a job. Others view them as non-feeling automaton-keepers-of-the-rules-and-regulations.

Desperate people tend to become familiar with all of the Human Resources staff as a means to obtain a position. The truly desperate and committed will call the Human Resources (HR) office at least once a week to keep their names on the minds of the staffing specialists.

Human Resources employees are human. They live lives, lose jobs, and face struggles. HR staff are required to deal in facts, and work with people from application status through retirement or death. HR staff have feelings—they just can't show it.

CHAPTER 1

Jenna Judkins was desperate for a job and needed to get this application submitted to the Human Resources office before midnight. She left her third job a few minutes early in order to submit her application before the deadline. Her bones were weary, her head pounded from the lack of sleep, and she couldn't remember the last time she had a meal. It seemed when she wasn't working, she was either traveling to or from a job. Her feet ached, and she didn't know how much longer she could keep up this killer schedule.

Jenna managed to piece together three part-time dead-end jobs, which only managed to meet some of her bills. Jenna was tired of always being a month or two behind on everything. She faced eviction and would probably ask one of her parents to help her out. Jenna was a college graduate with a marketing degree, and all she could find were jobs she refused to work in high school.

She just left her night custodian position with a contractor who cleaned several banks in the area. In a few hours, Jenna would have to report to her position at Harford Community College where she took notes for visually challenged students. Then she would have to make her way across Churchville Road to the McDonalds where she served as a cashier.

There was an opening for a Public Information Specialist with Nesbit Industries, one of the largest employers in Harford County. Jenna had a Bachelor's degree in business, a minor in marketing, and held several long term public relations internships. She was highly qualified and only needed an interview. Jenna felt once she showed them her portfolio of successful public relations campaigns, she was sure to get hired.

During her third year of college, Jenna was blessed with a paid internship with the Aberdeen Ironbirds minor league baseball team as an assistant to the public relations manager. She had a successful run for two seasons before the ball team announced layoffs. Last in, first out, and Jenna found herself scrambling for a job.

It was pitch black in the sky and it seemed there weren't any working street lights around, but Jenna didn't care. She had to beat the clock and needed to catch a break in the worst way.

Jenna's rent was due in two weeks, and unless she could convince her girlfriend Roxie to give her back the money she borrowed, she was going to lose her place. But if all else failed, she knew she could call her mom or dad.

It was 11:57 p.m. and she was still a block away. She knew that the evening custodian locked the mail slot at exactly midnight. Jenna raced to the parking lot. She parked her rusted 1987 Toyota Celica, affectionately known as "Road Beast." Her friends often teased her for driving the rusted car saying,

"Girl, you need a new car,"

Jenna would reply, "You know I don't believe in waste; this car still runs."

The Road Beast was her first car. She bought it while in high school and kept the maintenance up so although it wasn't much to look at, it was reliable and paid off.

Jenna ran up the steps to the door of the Human Resources office and noticed that the mail was still on the floor. Her palms were sweaty, and she could feel her heart beating in her chest to the drum of the veins in her neck.

"This is a sign from the Lord," she muttered as she shoved the application packet through the slot.

"Ewww! What is that junk on the slot?" she said to herself as she wiped the slimy gunk on her sweat stained uniform pants. She reached in her top jacket pocket for a tissue, she smelled the familiar metallic odor of blood. Jenna nearly fainted as she realized the sticky substance was actually blood.

What in the world? Jenna thought as she took a closer look at the mail slot. Jenna peered through the glass doors and banged on the glass.

"Mr. Johnson, are you okay?" Jenna jumped back from the front doors and pulled her cell phone out of her purse. She didn't spot any sign of Mr. Johnson and turned towards the street.

It was then that Jenna realized how late it was and how deserted the streets were. Peering out the corner of her eye, she began to move a little quicker and purposely to the car.

The moon moved farther away into the night sky and bathed the street in darkness.

As she moved toward the Road Beast, she spotted a large knife stuck in her tire.

"No!" Jenna screamed.

Quickly, she shut her mouth as she looked up and down the street. She frantically dialed 9-1-1 as she glanced around her and knelt down to look under her car.

"9-1-1, what is the nature of your emergency?"

"I'm at 201 South Hickory Avenue. There's blood on the door and someone cut my tire. I don't know what to do." Jenna rapidly spoke to the operator. She could barely keep her balance as she shook uncontrollably.

"Ms., please remain calm. We are sending a squad car to check it out."

Jenna disconnected the call and then dialed a familiar number.

"Hey, Pooka. What's going on?" asked Darius Judkins, Jenna's dad.

"Daddy, you will never believe what happened. I found some blood on the door and my tire has a knife in it!" Jenna became a little girl whenever she spoke to her dad. He always seemed to make everything better.

But as the tears began to pool in her eyes, she wasn't sure if he could fix this mess.

"Slow down and tell me what happened. Where are you?"

"I just dropped off my application over here at Human Resources." Jenna paced next to the car.

As she began to retell the tale of the night to her dad, the air around her appeared to shift.

Darius wracked his brain as he tried to figure out why his daughter was out at this time of night putting in applications. He realized that he didn't know which HR office she was near.

Jenna's conversation was cut short as she glimpsed a shadow out of the corner of her eye, which caused her to turn slightly to her right. As she turned, the shadow delivered a blow to her head.

She fell to the ground and dropped her cell phone near a pool of redness fingering its way toward the curb.

At the same time Jenna hit the ground, Darius' phone died.

"Jenna, what's that noise? What's going on? Hello? Hello?"

"God, please keep my baby safe. Show me what's going on." Darius said as he ran for his coat and keys. He was in such a rush to get to Jenna; he didn't realize he still had on his Sponge Bob pajama bottoms Jenna bought for him last Christmas.

"Hold on Pooka, I'm coming." Darius started his truck, plugged in his cell phone, and headed toward Bel Air.

As he made his way down Route 543, he dialed Gertrude, his ex-wife and Jenna's mom. "Hi, you've reached Gertrude; I'm not available right now. Please leave your name and number and I will get back to you."

Normally, Gertrude's happy sounding voicemail was a welcome sound, but Darius needed to speak to her. His priority was finding his daughter. *Where the heck is Gertrude, this time of night,* Darius thought.

Darius kept trying to reach Jenna with no success. He left a few messages and finally realized her phone must have died. *Why else wouldn't she answer when she needed him to come get her,* thought Darius.

Officer Theodore "Ted" Robertson was finishing up a report while sitting in his patrol car in the parking lot. His shift ended in fifteen minutes, and he was looking forward to going home. It had been a long day filled with misery, strife, and a lot of unnecessary drama.

He shifted in gear and slowly eased his way through the parking lot off of Main Street in Bel Air. When he turned to go towards the Sherriff's office, he spotted an animal lying near a car. He switched off the car and made his way to check it out. As he got closer, he realized it wasn't an animal but a woman lying in front of a car.

Ted felt for the woman's pulse and noted she still had life in her body. Her hand was at an awkward angle, but there didn't appear to be any other outward signs of trauma.

"Base, this is Robertson. I'm in the 200 block of Hickory Avenue, and I have a woman lying unconscious near a vehicle. I need paramedics."

"Roger that. We are sending them and backup," replied the dispatcher.

"Copy that." Ted drew his service piece, his flashlight, and began to look in the vehicle.

Ted began to quickly make his way back to the woman, he heard the sirens of the ambulance in the distance.

"Hold on Miss. Help is on the way," Ted said as he searched her pockets for a clue to her identity. The woman's head was facing sideways, and her hair was in her face. Ted didn't dare move her because he wasn't sure of her injuries.

"Let's see who you are Ms...." Ted said as he looked into the small billfold he found in her fleece jacket.

"Jenna Janice Judkins. Oh no..."

Ted realized he went to high school with the injured woman. At that moment an ambulance pulled up behind the Toyota, followed by a squad car. Two paramedics jumped out of the doors of the ambulance and didn't waste any time pulling out the stretcher and board.

They gently lifted the woman onto the board and maneuvered her head into a brace to keep her head from shifting as they lifted her into the back of the ambulance.

"We are taking her over to Upper Chesapeake Hospital off of Route 924 in Bel Air and should be there in a few minutes."

"Thanks, man," Ted said as he waved them off and put in a call to dispatch.

"Base, this is Robertson. The victim's name is Jenna Judkins; I knew the victim in high school. I've got her personal belongings and will follow the ambulance to the hospital."

"Roger that Robertson. We'll send the detectives out to the scene. Advise Officer Davis to secure the scene until the detectives get there."

Ted looked around the street and could not figure out how a sweet young lady like Jenna could find herself in this predicament. He wondered what happened to her in the years since high school and why someone stabbed her tire.

The Jenna he remembered was a straight "A" student, debate team champion, and the editor of their high school newspaper. She was always smiling, friendly to everyone, and always had a kind word to say to Ted.

He loved Jenna from a distance since their early days in elementary school. He was always the brunt of everyone's jokes, but Jenna was nice to him. It helped that she wasn't part of the "in" crowd because of her braces, exceptional height, and knobby knees.

All of that changed for her in high school when she grew into her body, became more comfortable with her subtle beauty, and seemed more confident.

Ted was always known as "Little Teddy" not only because of his short stature but also for his resemblance to the small, round fluffy creature. He was husky and often melted into the background.

All except Jenna; she went out of her way to try to include him in anything she was doing. Once she convinced Teddy to try out for the swim team. Both of them bombed miserably but enjoyed the adventure.

Ted remembered the summer Jenna talked him into making frozen cups of Kool-Aid and selling them for twenty-five cents. The pair of twelve-year-olds filled his mother's deep freezer with about four hundred cups. *The lines of children often went from the side door to the sidewalk and down the block. The only problem was adults and children didn't have respect for time and would often bang on the door at all hours of the night.*

"Hey little Teddy. You guys got any blue frozen cups?"

Bang. Bang. Bang. "I know you all hear me. I've been knocking for the last ten minutes. Just let me get a red and a blue. Ya'll got any honey buns?"

Ted's mom was understanding up to a point and shut their little enterprise down. Mrs. Williams didn't care about splitting $100 three ways. She wanted her sleep.

That was the summer he kissed Jenna, and to her surprise she liked it. The two of them were planning how to spend their earnings, and Teddy suggested they go to Kings Dominion. Jenna wanted to give 10 percent to the church and spend the rest buying school supplies for the less fortunate children in their middle school.

Ted looked into Jenna's excited face and caved in. He whispered the words she longed to hear. "Okay, Jenna. We'll do it your way."

To Ted's surprise, Jenna grabbed his head, pulled it to her, and planted a wet kiss right on his lips. She lingered a little longer than she intended. Ted thought he would pass out from both the surprise and the pleasure of the kiss.

"I'm sorry, Teddy. I didn't mean to do that. I better… I've gotta…" Jenna jumped up and ran across the street without looking back.

If she would've turned, she would've seen Little Teddy wearing a million dollar grin.

"Bye, Jenna. Call me."

Ted walked back to the patrol car. He noticed something by the right rear tire. He reached in his back pocket and pulled out a pair of latex gloves. He squatted down in order to get a better look.

Ted gently lifted the item and realized it was a cell phone battery. He could see the rest of the phone lying underneath the car.

Ted quickly walked around the car, lay in the street and reached his hand toward the cell phone pieces. He stood up, placed the battery in the phone, and turned it on. The cell phone screen remained dark.

He opened Jenna's car door and began to search the glove box for the car charger. He found a flashlight, sanitary napkins, lip gloss, and tissues.

"Here it is," Ted said.

Ted made his way back to the patrol car, plugged the phone into the car charger and sought the last caller. The last call was at 12:02 a.m. to "Daddy." As Ted dialed the number, he sent up a silent prayer.

"Lord, please heal Jenna and restore what was taken from her. Allow her to come through this situation better than she was before. Thank you for placing me here to find her. I don't know all that you are going to do, but I trust you. In Jesus name I pray, amen."

"Hey Pooka, it's Daddy, is everything okay?"

"Is this Mr. Judkins? This is Officer Theodore Robertson."

"Officer Robertson? What the heck is going on? Where is my daughter? How did you get her phone? Let me speak to Jenna please," Darius Judkins said as he began to panic as he drove the streets of Bel Air.

"Sir, I need you to remain calm. Ms. Judkins was taken to Upper Chesapeake Hospital. I'm following behind the ambulance."

"What the hell do you mean an ambulance? Somebody somewhere is going to pay if my baby girl has a scratch on her. I'm on my way. Thanks Officer," Darius yelled as he disconnected the call and reversed the car's direction.

Ted pulled into the emergency room parking lot, parked the police car and took a deep breath. He felt a sense of peace as he walked through the sliding glass doors. Everything was going to work out somehow.

CHAPTER 2

Gertrude Judkins looked at herself in her car's reflection and again realized she loved being tall. After forty-some-odd years of being this way, she accepted the fact that she was almost six feet tall. If only the people around her were that accepting.

"I can't believe you are that tall. Why do you wear heels?"

"How do you find pants that long?"

"Didn't they call you Lurch or Jolly Green Giant when you were growing up?"

That last comment or some other words to that effect, were often spoken by her mother. Ms. Betty, as she was affectionately known by all, was often brash in her retelling of Gertrude's height challenges during her childhood.

Ms. Betty was five feet even and couldn't understand why rehashing these stories to virtual strangers was humiliating for Gertrude.

If Gertrude brought it up, Ms. Betty accused Gertrude of being overly sensitive. So what was the point?

"Today is not the day to worry about such nonsense!" Gertrude murmured as she stepped out of her purple Chevy HHR.

Gertrude was fine-as-wine-in-the-sunshine and feeling herself this morning. She was wearing a fierce charcoal gray two piece skirt suit with matching grey patent leather sling backs. Her makeup was tastefully applied and a light spritz of Tom Ford Black Orchid trailed in her wake as she made her way up the block.

She acknowledged the two officers eyeing her from in front of the administration building.

"Good morning, gentlemen."

"How you doing, Miss?" said the shorter of the two.

"May I see your identification?" asked the finer, much taller one. He had to be six feet four inches and his complexion was just a little lighter than a Hershey Bar. Gertrude did like her chocolate.

"What's going on guys? I have negotiations this morning, and I need to get moving."

Gertrude was in a rush and needed to get into the building. She wanted to make certain she let herself into the negotiations room before the labor union representatives got there. Gertrude was a firm believer that the first person in the room controlled it, and there was no way, she was going to give up her edge to the union representatives.

Gertrude flashed her identification and attempted to squeeze between the two men. However, neither one of the men seemed eager to let her pass.

Mr. Hershey flashed his pearly whites at Gertrude and gave her outfit the once over. It appeared he approved of her coordinating pieces and gave a slight nod of acknowledgement.

"Mrs. Judkins, we are sorry for the inconvenience but unfortunately, all meetings have been cancelled."

Gertrude quickly scanned his identification badge. "Why is there such heavy security Officer Washington? Did someone die?"

"Why don't you go into the executive conference room and it will all be explained to you in a moment." Washington's face dimmed as he escorted Gertrude toward the front door.

As he placed his hand on the small of her back, Gertrude looked up into his eyes. It had been a long time since she had looked up at a man. It was a nice feeling. If only the feeling would last.

"Thank you for your help, Officer Washington," Gertrude said as she smiled at him.

"I only wish it was for something pleasant, Mrs. Judkins."

"I'm actually Ms. Judkins. Hopefully the next time it will be for something pleasant. Take care."

Officer Washington smiled as the confident woman breezed through the door. He wished he could have prevented the unpleasant situation awaiting her on the other side.

Gertrude walked into the door and suddenly got a bad feeling. The headache she worked so hard to leave at home suddenly began inching its icy fingers across her skull.

Whatever happened last night could not lead to good news this morning. Extra security, canceled meetings, and a headache meant there was a reason to pray in advance.

"Lord, please give me the strength to get through these next few moments. I pray for each of my coworkers. May they be safe and sound. I pray for the first responders. Give us peace in the midst of chaos. In your Son's name I pray, amen."

Gertrude made her way down the long hallway as her heels clicked along the marble tiles, which amplified the sound. She entered the glass doors of the conference room, Gertrude felt goose bumps along her spine. She recognized that feeling—she was in the presence of evil.

The muted whispers and quiet sobbing abruptly ceased as she entered the room. All eyes were on Gertrude as she took off her overcoat and took a seat closest to the door.

Gertrude looked around the room. Her nose and her brain were trying to place the familiar metallic odor in the room. Every woman knows that odor – the familiar metallic scent of blood and lots of it.

"Why would they bring us in here?" asked Miguel Fernandez, Human Resources Benefits Specialist. Miguel was chewing on his fingernail, pulling on his red tie, and fidgeting in his seat.

"What do you know?" Gertrude asked as she smoothed down her skirt.

"All I know is that there was blood in the hallways when I came in this morning," said Sonya Kennedy.

"Blood?" Gertrude looked around the conference room but was distracted by Sonya's appearance.

Sonya's normally greasy blond hair was pinned up and held by some sort of clip sticking out of her hair. Sonya always seemed to find the weirdest looking hairpins, bows, and other hair accessories. But somehow it worked for her.

Sonya was an HR Assistant when she joined the agency but didn't do well answering telephones or dealing with the public. She ended up in the file room but spent more time on the loading dock smoking than she did filing.

She often looked as if she needed a drink or cigarette but not necessarily in that order. No one could figure out how she kept her job for the last fifteen years since it seemed she couldn't alphabetize and often "lost" files in the file room.

Gertrude looked around the room at her fellow HR employees and tried to discover who was in attendance as well as who was missing.

"May I have your attention please? We know you all are wondering what has happened," said an older white gentleman with wavy, salt and pepper hair.

"My name is Detective Gentry and we are here to answer your questions. After I provide some information, each of you will be questioned by an officer in the order you came into the room."

Gertrude exhaled loudly. This was a day she was going to have to put under prayer cover. Detective Gentry walked around the room until he stood in front of the door. He tried to look sympathetic while making eye contact and assessing the odds of the perpetrator being in the room.

"I'm sorry to announce that two of your coworkers were found beaten and unconscious. A third employee is missing, and we believe she was kidnapped."

Gertrude looked over at Sonya and thought *if Sonya raises her hand and asks the obvious I'm going to pull off my shoe…*

"Excuse me sir, what does that mean exactly?" asked Sonya in that perpetually whiny voice of hers.

"It means two are in the hospital, and one was kidnapped, Chica," said Miguel.

Gertrude wondered why Miguel insisted on using that overly stereotypical Hispanic accent when he knew he grew up in Fallston where there are no Hispanics. His family kept the family name because of their burgeoning pharmaceutical company but lost the accents in the seventies.

Miguel was one of two benefits specialists in the HR office. He often went around bragging about his family's business and the fact that he didn't have to work. His run down shoes and worn clothes belied the fact he was worth millions.

Miguel actually loved his job and took the time with his clients. Last week he visited a dying custodian at her home in order to notarize beneficiary paperwork for her. It was his kindness to others that endeared him to Gertrude.

Detective Gentry said "Madeline Shaw and Worrell Stevens were found early this morning by the second shift custodian. We found a note that indicated Helena Perkins is being held against her will. We believe this was an isolated incident, but we'll conduct a thorough investigation."

Collective gasps went up around the room as employees shed tears and stared at each other in utter disbelief. All of her coworkers seemed shaken except Denise, who seemed confused.

Gertrude looked up to see who was sobbing loudly across from her, and made eye contact with Taurean Harris. He and Helena Perkins were engaged to be married. The former linebacker and the petite classification specialist had spent the last three months in premarital counseling as they prepared for the special day.

Helena shared a while back that although Taurean outweighed her by one hundred pounds and towered over her five feet nothing, she had him wrapped around her fingers. He was a big teddy bear who had saved himself for marriage. Five years of professional football and he walked away with his virginity and his salvation intact. Helena couldn't claim the virginity but had lived a celibate life for the last two years while dating Taurean. The wedding was less than two months away.

Kendra Walker was a staffing specialist who had over fifteen years with the agency and was good at her job. She had the knack for recruiting talented IT professionals away from Fortune 500 companies and placing them in positions with the agency. Kendra also managed to attract the attention of every virile male within the agency. She dressed provocatively and flirted daily with dress code violations.

Today Kendra was dressed in a frilly, lime green top, which gave the casual observer pause, due to the amount of cleavage spilling out of the top. Her skirt was just above the knee but hugged her generous bottom and emphasized her curvy figure. A pair of lime green Jimmy Choos pumps set off the outfit.

Kendra was rubbing her hands over Taurean's back offering comfort and a little something else. It was no secret that she wanted Taurean and the purported millions of dollars he stashed away. She was a gold digger and was very proud of that fact. With her killer curves, luscious mouth, and eager to please attitude, she kept many a man on the bench waiting to be called up to the majors.

Gertrude began to pray "*God please don't let that… young lady tempt Taurean. I lift him up to you now and pray that you minister to his heart and soul. Bring him comfort during this hard time, in Jesus' name, amen.*"

As Gertrude finished her prayer, she felt the eyes of Stan Winters on her. She didn't know why she always knew when he was looking, but she always felt dirty afterward.

Stan was a little too slick, a little too something, and he often trifled with women yet claimed to be living right. He would stare at women in hopes of catching a glimpse of flesh. Gertrude caught him looking at her one time like he was trying to mind-meld her button-up shirt open.

Stan and Gertrude attended the same church, but sometime soon Gertrude was going to find a new place to worship. She and Stan grew up together in Harford County and were often in each other's classes all throughout high school. They never dated but often had common friends and ran into each other at parties, games, and church functions.

Stan's parents were divorced, but they worshipped in the same church. His parents sat in different pews and ignored each other. Stan's family was weird in an Addams family kind of way. Maybe it was due to the fact they owned several funeral homes.

Gertrude remembered in fifth grade Stan told her, "I can fit your body in two jars." She didn't know what that meant, but Stan never forgot the black eye she gave him for yelling it across the school yard. Gertrude gladly took a beating from her mom for wiping the smirk off his round little face.

Rachel was giving Gertrude the eye from across the room. When she bowed her head, Gertrude knew that was the signal to begin praying over the situation.

Gertrude smiled at her coworker and good friend, Rachel Ward. Rachel was as short as Gertrude was tall. They often associated outside of work, and Gertrude knew that Rachel was a practicing Christian who always had her back. It was hard to find a sister who was friendly, knowledgeable, and didn't want to steal your job, your man, or your weave!

Rachel was good people with a short temper and often had to repent and pray for some of her comments. The two of them together could cut the fool! Many days they laughed and cried over some of life's crazy moments.

But Rachel looked worn down. Her normally neat locks looked dusty and dry. Gertrude wondered if Rachel had eaten her breakfast or if the baby was stressing her body. Rachel and her husband John had tried for four years to get pregnant without success. When they finally quit trying, they received their miracle. Gertrude would have to keep an eye on her.

In her mind, Gertrude was warring in the heavenlies, leaving no one uncovered, and asking God's wisdom in the midst of the trial. As she finished her prayers, she took comfort in knowing God was still God and in control of all.

"I was praying, too, just so you know," Denise whispered softly. "I often find that God brings peace in the middle of my chaos if I pray."

Denise Krapel was an older, mousy woman who kept to herself. It worked for her since she generated reports and vast amounts of research for other departments but didn't have to make any presentations. Denise didn't like to make eye contact and preferred the solitude of her office.

Gertrude could not have been any more surprised by Denise's announcement if it came from heaven itself. In the five years since Gertrude joined the company, Denise never once mentioned God or prayer. Come to think of it, that may have been the most she had ever spoken aloud in Gertrude's presence.

Gertrude's smile brightened as she realized Denise was indeed a saint of God. "I'm glad you're praying. I just hope everyone will be okay."

Denise nodded and moseyed over to a chair in the corner far away from the others.

The morning seemed to drag as the officers called each of the employees into the interview room. One-by-one the employees walked out withdrawn and mentally scarred. Gertrude eyed each one as they gathered their belongings and made their way to the suite of offices.

This was a day straight out of the pits of hell.

CHAPTER 3

Darius Judkins was a good-looking man. But the tight-lipped nurse sitting in front of him was not impressed with his male model looks and refused to go along with his flattery to get the info program.

"Sir, I've already explained that we cannot release any information on Ms. Jenna Judkins, so please stop asking," the nurse stated firmly.

"I can understand you've had a rough shift, and are probably a little tired as well as in need of some gentle affection."

The nurse's harsh features began to soften as she thought this man might be the answer to one of her many prayers. She always did like a man with a fresh haircut and who was well groomed.

This specimen standing in front of her was licking his lips like L.L. Cool J, the rapper, and his lips were juicier than L.L's lips. Her mind began to drift, her mouth opened slightly, and she began to speak the words Darius needed to hear.

Darius softly hummed an old L.L. Cool J song.

"Your daughter is in room 209, but she is under police guard. I will call back there and let them know you are on your way back."

Darius flashed his straight white teeth at the woman and licked his lips.

"Thanks. I may just have to stop by on my way out and work out that kink in your neck." He winked as he moved toward the end of the hall.

"My name is Sabrina; I get off in a couple of hours. Why don't we hookup later?"

Darius pretended he didn't hear those last comments as he made his way toward the elevator. He needed to get to Jenna's room as soon as possible.

Darius hated hospitals and all that went with them. He couldn't stomach blood. The antiseptic smell began to mess with his stomach and was giving him a bad case of bubble guts.

He found room 209. The police officer was missing from in front of Jenna's door. He walked into the room and made his way toward the policeman sitting in a chair close to Jenna's bed.

Darius cleared his throat at the same time the officer put his hand on his service weapon.

"Sir, how may I help you?" asked the officer as he stood up.

"This is my daughter." Darius cautiously approached the bed with his hand extended toward the officer.

As they shook hands, Darius noted the officer's attention was still on his daughter.

"Do you know Jenna?"

"We used to go to the same high school, sir. My name is Officer Robertson, Ted Robertson, sir."

Darius focused on the young man's face. He recognized the once geeky, little boy from down the street. It seemed the pudgy, little boy with the thick glasses had grown into quite the man.

"Little Teddy?"

"Yes sir, that's me," Ted said, chuckling.

Darius approached the hospital bed with leaden footsteps. He couldn't believe that his precious baby girl was in the hospital. Darius almost fainted as he looked at all of the tubes, wires, and monitors attached to Jenna. The beeps and whirs let him know that the situation was serious.

"I was in my truck and realized I left my wallet in the house," Darius began. "I jumped back in my truck and was down the block when the phone rang. It was an officer telling me that Jenna was in the hospital. I tried not to wrap it around a pole on my way here." Darius gently reached for Jenna's hand and realized he never noticed she had her mother's long fingers.

"Sir, I'm the officer that called you."

A firm knock sounded on the door as a doctor walked in. "I'm Doctor Black, the attending physician. Are you a relative of Ms. Judkins?"

"I'm her father, Darius Judkins. How is my baby girl?" he asked.

"Ms. Judkins has suffered a slight head injury as a result of blunt force trauma to the back of the head. She has some contusions along her chest and fractured her wrist apparently while falling. She is lucky she was found not long after the incident. Her vitals are strong."

Dr. Black's calm demeanor soothed Darius. "Is she in a coma?" Darius whispered.

"No, she is just resting from the pain medicine. We did have to monitor her closely for the possibility of swelling of the brain but the scans do not show any swelling at this time," said Dr. Black.

He walked around checking the monitors and moved over to the computer and entered his notes into the system.

"Ms. Judkins should wake up in a few hours or so," he said when he noticed Darius staring at him. "We will do what we can to keep her comfortable and will probably keep her for another twenty four hours just to be safe."

"Thanks, Dr. Black," Darius said as he shook the doctors hand.

Darius walked back to the bed and whispered, "I love you Pooka. I'm so glad you are safe. I almost lost my mind when my phone died. I didn't know what happened to you."

Darius scraped the chair across the floor and took Jenna's hands. He prayed.

"Lord, thank you so much for rescuing my baby girl. She is the joy of my life, and I don't know what I would've done if it turned out differently.

You are Jehovah Rapha, our healer, and I ask you to heal her body, her mind, and her spirit. Renew her, refresh her, and restore her.

I thank you for all these things in Jesus' name, amen."

Ted walked out of the room and waited for the police guard to return. Ted knew he violated procedure by even being in front of the room, but he had to make sure Jenna was okay. His countenance brightened as he realized Jenna wasn't seriously hurt. A smile began to form on his face as he sent up a prayer of thanks.

He thanked God for sending him down the street where Jenna laid in front of her car. He thanked Him for keeping her safe. Most of all he thanked Him for allowing Ted to have another chance with Jenna. He thought of her often throughout his college years but always seemed to miss her when she returned to her parents' home during breaks.

Officer Allen returned to the door with a bottle of water. "Thanks for covering the room for me so I could get a quick drink. Is she okay?"

"Ms. Judkins' father just arrived. It seems she is resting comfortably. I better get out of here before I get written up." Ted offered his hand to shake Officer Allen's hand.

"Thanks again, Allen."

"I'll keep an eye on her. We won't let anything else happen to your friend."

Ted made his way down the hall and wondered about Mrs. Judkins. From what he remembered of the woman, he couldn't believe she wasn't here with her daughter.

The noon day sun was fading, and a slight breeze ruffled the leaves as Officer Robertson walked toward his car. Again his thoughts turned to the young lady on the second floor of the hospital. It was a bittersweet moment.

He often wanted to be the man to rescue Jenna when they were in high school and here he had rescued her, but she wasn't aware of it. He would take back those wishes if it meant Jenna would be okay.

CHAPTER 4

Kendra's three-inch heels clicked as she walked along the tile floors. Her gait was unsteady, and her footsteps were unsure as she made her way to the ladies room. Her stomach soured and sent up a noxious fume to her parched throat causing her to gag.

The bubble guts were getting worse, and she wasn't sure if she would make it without letting out explosive gases. She burped a little and almost threw up the honey nut granola bar and latte she scarfed down on the way to work. Sweat beads were forming along her nose and forehead.

Biting her lips, she pushed inside the restroom and headed to the nearest stall.

Stan couldn't wait until he was released from the interview to make his way down the hall. As anticipation filled his heart, his lips began to spread in a leer as the sweat pooled on his nose and forehead. He quickly took a look down the long hallway and glanced over his shoulders to make certain he was not spotted as he entered the electric closet.

Stan just happened to walk into the closet one day to see if he tripped a circuit and heard female laughter. Unbeknownst to his coworkers, Stan had found out that the closet had a hole in the wall that allowed an unrestricted view into the handicapped stall of the women's restroom.

He was able to view a woman's private time for the last two years without discovery and became bolder each time. Stan drilled small holes along the same wall to be able to see in the other three stalls.

Stan watched Kendra walk out of the conference room and had a feeling she was going to the bathroom.

Stan looked at Kendra's silky lace underwear and wanted to reach out and touch her. He wished Kendra noticed him and would allow him to be her man. He knew how to treat a woman because he read all of the romance novels they liked and watched the chick flicks on television. He memorized classic pick-up lines from each one and tried them out on the women he met at church. They weren't in the same class as Kendra, but they served a purpose until Kendra would see the error of her ways and make Stan her man.

As Stan continued to spy on Kendra, he noticed her graying pallor. She didn't look well and seemed unsure on her feet. As she trembled uncontrollably, her last conscious thought was *oh crap* before she hit the floor.

Before Stan could blink, he watched Kendra fall to the ground.

Without thinking he beat his feet and burst through the women's restroom door. He picked up Kendra, gently pulled up her underclothes and ran to the conference room.

"Call 9-1-1 quick!" Stan yelled as he ran down the hallway. Detective Gentry was just stepping into the hallway when he noticed Stan.

"What's going on Mr. Winters?" Detective Gentry asked as he radioed to dispatch for an ambulance.

"I heard a loud noise when I walked past the door of the restroom. I ran inside and found her passed out on the floor," Stan said. He was having trouble breathing as he noticed Kendra began trembling violently and making hacking sounds.

"Put her on the floor so I can begin CPR."

As Detective Gentry began CPR, a crowd began to form as Kendra's coworkers stood around unable to believe the events of the morning.

Gertrude, Denise, Rachel and Taurean slipped into the conference room and formed a prayer circle. The group took turns lifting up Kendra before the throne of God praying for her speedy healing and her general wellbeing.

"I don't know how much more of this I can take. First Helena is missing, Worrell and Madeline are hospitalized," Taurean moaned.

Rachel rubbed Taurean's back and offered a silent prayer. "Where the heck is the ambulance?" she said.

As soon as she uttered the phrase, the wailing siren sounded in the distance.

As they made their way out of the conference room with heavy hearts and minds, Gertrude realized that the full group wasn't in attendance.

"Where are Miguel and Sonya? Normally they don't miss the chance for some juicy gossip."

The paramedics burst through the front door hurling a stretcher toward the group. As one paramedic lifted and strapped Kendra on the stretcher, the other one was asking Detective Gentry questions. They quickly strapped an oxygen mask and blood pressure cuff on her as they raced out to the ambulance.

"I'm going with her," said Stan as he grabbed his jacket and followed the stretcher to the ambulance.

"Are you family?" the bulky paramedic asked.

"I'm the only family she's got," Stan said as he closed the door. The ambulance raced off to Upper Chesapeake, the nearest hospital.

"No one is to leave this room until we understand what is going on here," Detective Gentry announced as he walked toward the glass doors.

Gertrude reached for her cell phone inside her large purse. She fished around for it and could feel the phone vibrating at the bottom of her purse.

She looked at the screen and noticed she had fifteen missed calls and several text messages. She scrolled through the messages and all were from Darius. She almost deleted them until she saw the words "Jenna" and "hospital." Almost in a near panic she dialed the voice mail.

"Hey babe. Our baby girl is in the hospital. She is okay; just a fractured wrist and some bumps and bruises. Jenna is in room 209 at Upper Chesapeake. I'm here with her."

"Oh God!" Gertrude screamed. Tears pooled in her eyes as Gertrude quickly grabbed her things and made her way toward the policemen standing outside of the conference room.

"Excuse me gentlemen. I must leave because of a family emergency," Gertrude calmly but forcefully said.

Officer Washington made his way toward Gertrude and placed his hand on the small of her back. "I just got the call from the station. I will drive you to Upper Chesapeake to see about your daughter."

"Thank you so much."

Officer Washington escorted Gertrude toward his unmarked vehicle. He opened the door for her as she slid inside. He couldn't help but to admire her long, luscious legs as he closed the door. Under other circumstances, Officer Washington would have asked her out. But now was not the time nor the place.

Gertrude wondered how Jenna's ended up at the hospital again. Her daughter was as clumsy as they came, but she hadn't ever fractured anything.

Jenna had about ten or twelve pairs of crutches, braces, and canes from all of the previous trips to emergency rooms. One time she fell and broke three toes while trying out for the track team.

This was just another one of those moments that the three of them would laugh about later.

Gertrude took a look at the dashboard clock; it was almost one in the afternoon. This day couldn't end fast enough. She had enough excitement in the last few hours than she could stand.

Officer Washington turned the car into the emergency room parking lot. He glanced over at Gertrude. He saw the frown lines in Gertrude's brow relax and heard her breathing slow down to a normal rhythm.

"I hope all is well with your daughter, Ms. Judkins."

"Thanks for driving me to the hospital. You've gone above and beyond the call of duty." Gertrude said as she unbuckled her seat belt.

Officer Washington quickly made his way around the car, opened the door, and offered Gertrude his hand to assist her out of the vehicle.

"Thanks again for your help, Officer Washington."

"You take care, Ms. Judkins."

Gertrude made her way to the elevators as a group of nurses made its way off.

"Girl, I'm telling you, that guy had the juiciest lips. He was so fine and he was feeling me," said the one on the right.

Gertrude pressed the second floor button and tapped her foot as she waited for the ding of her arrival. She realized that Darius' message didn't leave a whole lot of information beyond the fact that she wasn't really hurt. Gertrude wondered who drove Jenna to the hospital. She knew it wasn't that so-called friend Roxie.

She couldn't understand the friendship between the two. Jenna was a soft-hearted, kind, young woman who believed everything she was told. She wanted to see the best in people and often overlooked the fact that her friendships were a little one-sided.

Roxie, as Gertrude recalled, became a friend to Jenna as a means to an end. Jenna had money; Roxie's family was broke and often hustled to scrape enough money for the drugs they liked to smoke, snort, or whatever else they did. Gertrude wasn't a snob. She came from humble beginnings and thanks to two worthless ex-husbands, knew what it was like to struggle. It took her several years to get to a place where she wasn't living paycheck to paycheck.

Something about Roxie never rang true with Gertrude. When the two girls were in junior high school, Roxie just seemed to be too street—too something—a little too slick. Her lips said she was Jenna's best friend, but sometimes Gertrude caught Roxie looking at Jenna in a way that scared her.

Gertrude was smart enough to know that forbidding the friendship was the quickest way to seal that snake to Jenna. All she could do was surround her daughter with prayers and bind up the evil plans that Roxie tried to rope Jenna into.

How long does it take a stupid elevator to go up two floors? Gertrude thought. She was becoming anxious. It may be due to the fact her ex-husband Darius was in close proximity. The man both attracted and repelled her at the same time.

Gertrude couldn't deny their chemistry, but her mind knew that messing with him was like holding a rattlesnake. They both could hypnotize you with their tails, but the end result was a slow, painful death. Gertrude giggled as she thought maybe the death part was an exaggeration, but it was close to the truth. She loved Darius, but they were better for each other apart.

The elevator doors opened up, and Gertrude made her way down the hall. She looked at the door signs, she realized there was a police officer in front of the door of 209.

"Oh Jesus, what is going on," Gertrude cried as she ran toward the door just as it opened, and Darius walked out.

"I heard you coming down the hall. Calm down baby. Jenna is fine."

"Why is there a police officer if she is fine, Darius?"

"Let's take a walk and I will tell you what I know."

"Darius, I'm not moving from this spot until you tell me why there is an officer in front of my baby's door!" Gertrude's eyes filled with tears, and her lip quivered as she looked at Darius.

Darius was always moved by Gertrude's tears. The ten years since they parted ways had not changed the way she moved him. He always wanted to slay whatever made her cry.

Darius gently took hold of her hand and guided her toward the chairs opposite Jenna's room. He pulled out a tissue from his pocket and wiped her tears.

"I was talking to Jenna last night..."

"Last night? Are you telling me our daughter has been here all night and I'm just finding out?" Gertrude launched to her feet and began to pace.

Darius knew from experience to quit talking at this point. His ex-wife had to put everything in date and time order before he continued. As she did in her job, she reviewed all the facts in her mind before allowing Darius to proceed. He would wait for the questioning to begin.

"Darius, what time were you talking to Jenna?"

"About midnight or so…"

"What was going on? Why were you talking to her so late?"

"Jenna's tire had a knife in it and she called me in a panic."

"A knife in her tire," Gertrude repeated slowly as she sank back into her chair.

"Babe, our daughter is fine. She has a few contusions and a fractured wrist but is resting comfortably."

"Where is Roxie? Didn't she drive Jenna?"

"An ambulance drove her. If you let me finish the story, you will have all the information I have."

Darius told her about Jenna's incident while studying Gertrude closely.

"Thank you for being here for our daughter. I want to see her now."

"She's heavily medicated, so she's still probably asleep."

"I think our girl will be sitting up when we walk in there," Gertrude said matter-of-factly.

As they headed back toward the room, Officer Allen stopped them mid-stride.

"Mr. Judkins, only family is allowed in here," Officer Allen said.

"Hi, Officer, my name is Gertrude Judkins, I'm the mother."

"Oh, I'm sorry ma'am. You look too young to be her mother. I apologize."

Darius rolled his eyes and opened the door.

"You still got these brothers using those pickup lines on you, Gert."

"Don't be mad because everyone thinks you're the oldest." Gertrude smirked; she was six years older than Darius, yet everyone thought he was older.

Gertrude's smile brightened as she walked into the room and spotted her baby girl sitting up in bed, watching TV.

"How's my girl?" Gertrude took two quick steps and was in front of the bed gently hugging Jenna.

"I'm fine. My head hurts and my hand feels like somebody hit it with a sledge hammer."

"Hey Pooka," Darius said. He leaned over and kissed her forehead.

"Daddy, I can't believe this happened. I don't know why someone would hit me in the back of the head."

"Hit in the head? Darius, you didn't tell me she was attacked!"

"Gertrude, I did tell you everything, but you blocked out most of what I said just like always. Then you find a way to turn it around and make it my fault." Darius huffed and walked over to the chair in the corner.

"That's not what I meant. You told me she hit her head, not that someone hit her in it. Those details are important to try to figure out what happened."

"This is not one of your murder mystery books, Gertrude. Please let the professionals handle this. You always want to investigate everything."

"I believe in getting to the truth, Darius. Things have to add up to make sense."

"Sometimes you just have to have faith, Gert," Darius said as his demeanor changed, and he sank further into the seat.

"So tell me daughter-of-mine, what were you doing out at almost midnight?"

"I was going to apply for the Public Information Specialist position at Nesbit Industries. I got extra hours cleaning so I didn't get a chance to drop it off until right before the dropbox closed at midnight. I couldn't take off from work so I needed to get it there."

"Jenna, do you have any idea how dangerous that is…"

Jenna hung her head and softly cried.

"Oh, honey, I'm sorry. Are you okay?"

Gertrude scooted the chair so she could see both Jenna and Darius. The fluorescent lights were subdued and the overcast sky cast an eerie glow into the room.

Jenna yawned and stretched her one good arm over her head. Her eyelids fluttered closed as she sank into the pillows.

"Honey, why don't you lie down and get some rest while your father and I go look for something to drink."

Just as Gertrude stood up, a nurse walked in. "Good afternoon, I'm here to check Ms. Judkins' vitals."

Gertrude noticed the nurse cast a long side glance at Darius, but his attention was focused on Jenna. Gertrude was glad that Jenna was his priority these days. During the years leading up to their divorce and the years since, Darius spent most of his time chasing women. His daughter was low on the totem pole.

The father-daughter relationship improved once Jenna went off to college.

"Darius, make sure you stop by the nurse' station on your way home. You promised to take care of my aching neck." The nurse swiveled in Darius' direction and grinned at him.

Gertrude kept walking, shook her head, and thought, *some things never change.*

"No problem, young lady. My wife and I will stop by and see you on the way out," Darius said. He chuckled and placed his hand on the small of Gertrude's back.

"Why did you say I'm your wife? My man could be working in this hospital. You know how gossip gets started."

Gertrude couldn't believe Darius was still playing childish games with grown women.

"This is why we're divorced. You should use your powers of persuasion for good, not evil."

"Only on you, Boo. You know my heart will always belong to you." His voice deepened with the dimples in his cheeks.

"Don't start that mess. It was never your heart I had a problem with, it was your non-committed body parts!" Gertrude cringed as she realized how loud and emotional she had gotten. Lately Darius always seemed to try to get a rise out of her, and he managed to get under her skin again.

"I'm sorry Darius; I didn't mean to say it like that. I'm over us and just wish you wouldn't include me in your childish games with other women. It's disrespectful and rude."

Darius' eyes softened as he realized he hurt Gertrude. He was so often off of his game whenever he was around her. Darius resorted to the kind of man she couldn't stand rather than take the chance to be open and honest about his unresolved feelings for his Gert.

"You are right as always Gert. I apologize. Why did you want to step outside? Our baby girl just woke up, and you ran out of there."

"I didn't want Jenna to hear us talking. Tell me more about the attack. Did the officer tell you what she was hit with? What time was it when they found her? I didn't get a chance to tell you they found two of my coworkers beaten unconscious in the office this morning. Helena Perkins was kidnapped. I'm wondering if Jenna witnessed anything," Gertrude said without taking a breath.

"Gert, don't go into investigation mode. I told you to let the police handle it."

"Darius, you forget we are no longer married; you are not the boss of me! I will talk to Jenna and find out what she knows." Gertrude stuck out her tongue as she walked down the hall back toward Jenna's room.

"Gert, I'm not playing with you. Get back here!" Darius marched down the hall following the trail of Tom Ford perfume and watched her hips sway. He couldn't help but smile when he remembered the night he bought her first bottle of Tom Ford and the way her body thanked him.

"Gert, I mean it," Darius called out, but her long legs carried her into the room before the sound of his voice could reach her.

It was going to be a long, long night, Darius thought as he walked into the room that held his two favorite women.

"Mom, have you heard from Roxie?" Jenna asked, "She was supposed to meet me at the house Friday and I haven't heard from her."

"I haven't seen Roxie around lately. Did you check your cell phone?"

"Officer Robertson was here earlier, and he put your stuff in a bag," said Darius. He walked over to the small closet at the rear of the room. He pulled out a small plastic bag and found several items but no cell phone.

"Pooka, it's not in here. Maybe Officer Robertson has it. He probably needs a reason to stop by and see you when you wake up."

"Why would an officer need a reason to stop by?" Gertrude asked.

"Oh snap! You guys will never guess who Officer Robertson really is…it's little Teddy!!"

"You've got to be kidding me!" Gertrude said. "I always liked him. He was always following behind Jenna."

"Mom, that is so not true. We were just friends, nothing more."

"Darling, that young man wanted to be more than your friend; you were just too blind to see it. Darius, what's he look like now? Is he still short and round?"

"Nope. He's about six feet six inches and almost three hundred solid! I had to look up at the brother!"

Gertrude almost said something sarcastic but changed her mind. Darius was five feet nine to Gertrude's six feet and height was a sensitive subject for him.

"Well…" Jenna yawned and gently closed her eyes.

Darius walked over and placed a kiss on her forehead while Gertrude pulled the blanket up over her shoulders. Darius dimmed the lights and grabbed Gertrude's purse from the back of the chair.

"Come on Gert. Let's go get something to eat while our baby sleeps."

"I don't know if I want to be seen with you while your stalker is roaming the halls," Gertrude said, laughing as she followed Darius out the door.

"Stop playing Gert. I ain't thinking about that girl."

"Well your girlfriend has decided she's thinking about you. I'll talk to her. What's her name?"

"Sandy, Sabrina, oh hell, I don't remember."

"Excuse me Ms., I'm Darius's ex-wife, and I just want to ask a small favor on his behalf. Would you please take extra special care of his daughter for him? He'd like that very much."

Gertrude could barely contain the laughter bubbling inside her. It would serve Darius right if he couldn't shake little Ms. Sunshine for the rest of the evening. It would give her a chance to make a few calls to see what she could find out about the cases.

As Gertrude waited, the elevator suddenly opened to reveal Officer Washington dressed in casual clothing.

"Ms. Judkins, I was hoping to catch you here. The detective handling the case wanted you brought in for questioning. I'm here to escort you to the station."

"Well, Officer Washington, thank you for the escort. My daughter is resting comfortably and I was just on my way to get a snack in the cafeteria."

"Please call me Jax, short for Jackson."

"Only if you call me Gertrude. So Jax, how is it you are the one taking me back to the station? Aren't you off work?"

"Truth be told, I volunteered to come get you. I figured you were still here and it would give us a chance to…" Jax was interrupted before he could finish speaking.

"Give you a chance to do what?" Darius asked. "Just what is going on Gert? Our daughter is laying in here almost on life support, and you are picking up men," Darius said. He paced in front of the couple.

"Ms. Judkins, who is this gentleman? Sir, I'm Officer Jax Washington and I'm taking Ms. Judkins down to the station for questioning. We only let her leave work to check on her daughter, but we need to get going."

"Darius, why don't you go back to the room and stay with Jenna while I go with this nice gentleman to the station. Besides, aren't you supposed to hook up with Sabrina? She's over there at the nurses' station staring us down." Gertrude pointed to the young woman.

"Gert, we are going to talk about this later. Officer." Darius stomped down the hall past the nurse as she attempted to get his attention. Sabrina trailed behind him speaking softly but soon realized Darius was not going to stop.

Jax pushed the down button as he tried to slow his heart rate. Something about this woman was making him excited, nervous, and a little off-center, but he liked it. Since meeting her this morning, he wanted to be in her presence.

Gertrude looked up at Jax and couldn't help smiling. He was very handsome, but there was something else she couldn't quite put her finger on it. He was calm in the midst of chaos and seemed to have a very gentle manner. She was intrigued by him and felt very comfortable in his presence, which was strange for her.

Normally Gertrude tried to figure a person out, determine the weakness, and place them in the friend or foe pile in her organized mind. However, there didn't seem to be a category for him.

"Jax, how long do you think this is going to take?" Gertrude asked as she stepped in the waiting elevator.

Jax pressed the first floor button. "It depends on the detectives. It's best to cooperate and provide any information you think they need."

"Do you know anything about Jenna's case?"

"No, I haven't heard anything beyond what you know. I haven't seen Officer Robertson. I heard he discovered the body… I mean your daughter."

"I'm just glad she is alive. I can't believe Officer Robertson is little Teddy from down the street. What a small world."

"You know Ted? I mentored him when he first came on the force. He's a good kid. A little serious sometimes, but a fine officer."

"I can believe it. Teddy was a smart young man and a good friend to Jenna."

"Ms. Judkins…"

"Please call me Gertrude." She walked off the elevator toward the double glass doors.

"Gertrude, I'm sorry about your daughter and your coworkers. It's been a rough day for you."

"I appreciate you coming all this way to escort me back. You've had a long shift as well."

Jax looked around the darkened parking lot as he opened the passenger door of his Chevy Avalanche truck.

Classical music gently played in the background as the pair rode through the streets of Bel Air.

"I love classical music. It keeps me calm throughout my day no matter what is going on in the office," Gertrude said. She nodded her head slowly to the beat of the music.

"I do love all kinds of music—jazz, classical, slow jams—you name it."

"Do you play an instrument?" Gertrude asked as they pulled up to the station parking lot.

"Jax, where have you been?" an officer yelled as Jax hopped out of his truck. "We've been trying to reach you for the last half hour."

As Jax made his way around the truck to open the door for Gertrude, he explained his whereabouts.

Standing in front of Gertrude, Jax fixed his attention on getting her out of his truck. She allowed him to lead her from the doorway; he placed his hand on her back and guided her up the short staircase. Jax acknowledged the stares and greetings of his coworkers as they entered the chaos of the precinct.

Jax led Gertrude down a narrow walkway in between cubicles toward a conference room. He knocked on the door, pushed it open, walked Gertrude in and sat her at a small table. After a few moments, Detective Gentry walked in followed by a small framed woman whom seemed to have an attitude problem.

"Mrs. Judkins, I'm Detective Betancourt, and I believe you've already met Detective Gentry," she said as she offered her hand and her business card. "We need to ask you a few questions but wish to advise you of your rights."

"My rights? I thought I was just being asked a few questions like my coworkers? Am I under arrest? Jax, what the hell is going on?"

"Officer Washington is leaving. He's off duty and should not be here. We do appreciate him bringing you in, but his responsibility ends right now."

"Gertrude, here's my card with all of my contact information. Call me when you're done, and I will pick you up."

"Oh no, Officer Washington I believe you've done enough. I don't need your kind of help. Wow. Simple me, I thought you were trying to help me—not deliver me like some kind of Judas!"

CHAPTER 5

Roxie Vega looked up and down the alleyway before heading toward the nearest dumpster. She peered around the opposite side and glanced furtively up the alleyway. She listened for a car engine, and when she didn't hear one, placed her hands on the crusted dumpster and pulled herself over the side. She glanced at the relatively empty dumpster and landed on top of the heap. She didn't hear any rodents and figured she could rest a while.

This was not the way she pictured her day when she woke up yesterday morning. Roxie knew she was in big trouble and didn't have any idea how she was going to get out of this mess. All she knew was she wasn't safe at her house. She was wearing the same clothes she had on Friday as she was on her way to Jenna's house. Someone followed her so she didn't stop by Jenna's house as she intended.

"Oh snap!" Roxie said. "What was I thinking? I'll call Jenna and she'll let me crash at her house for a few."

Just as quickly as the thought entered her head, she released it. Jenna didn't deserve to get caught up in this mess. Roxie had to learn to stand on her own two feet. Jenna was green as grass and didn't understand the streets.

Roxie grew up in the projects of New York City and was happy as hell when her mom dragged her to Baltimore. Compared to where she grew up, living in Baltimore was a piece of cake. Her mom's sister died and left them a row home in Edison-Belair. They didn't have much money, but her mom was a natural born hustler who believed in getting what she needed at all costs, including selling her young pre-teen daughter to get it. That was a road Roxie didn't wish to revisit, but her mind insisted.

She had gotten pulled out of a rat trap basement with some old guy who had three bags of heroin on him. The cops figured out pretty quickly Roxie wasn't an adult and contacted her mom. When they pulled up to the house, Roxie knew something was wrong because the front door was wide open. The officer pulled his weapon and entered the home leaving Roxie on the porch. When he returned moments later, Roxie knew in her heart her mom had died. She didn't wait for the officer to give the speech she had heard other officers give her friends.

"Where am I going to go? I don't want to be in foster care out here."

"I'll take you to a spot I know that takes teens. But you better listen to what they tell you to do or you'll find yourself back on this same block."

Roxie was placed in a foster home in Aberdeen. On her first day at Aberdeen Middle, she literally bumped into Jenna Judkins. Jenna was a tall girl with buck teeth, thick glasses, and a genuine designer bag. Roxie knew quality and money when she saw it. She immediately became Jenna's best friend, protector, and confidante.

In return Jenna offered Roxie a surrogate family, designer clothes, and an endless supply of food. Roxie could not believe that Jenna would open her life up to her and allow her to be a part of it. For that, Roxie was her friend for life, although Ms. Gertrude, Jenna's mom, didn't trust her.

Roxie was actually afraid of getting on Ms. Gertrude's bad side. That woman had the nose of a bloodhound and could sniff out a lie the way a drug sniffing dog sniffed out marijuana in a tractor trailer filled with coffee beans. Ms. Gertrude didn't play, and she certainly didn't trust her. Roxie just wished she would give her a chance. Jenna's mom made snide little remarks around her and about her.

Jenna's mom had no idea of the amount of trouble she kept Jenna from. Roxie spent her high school years blocking the football and basketball players from trying to capture Jenna's virginity. Of course Roxie offered herself to the players in Jenna's place. She knew they didn't really care for her, but it was her way to shield Jenna from the riffraff walking the halls of Harford Technical High School.

Roxie couldn't believe she let Jenna talk her into applying for Harford Tech. Four years later, she couldn't believe it when she walked across the stage to receive her diploma and a full scholarship to Harford Community College's Pre-Nursing degree program. She owed it all to Jenna's encouragement and constant nagging. Roxie loved Jenna, and she was the only family Roxie had left.

Roxie focused on her surroundings and noticed the sun had gone down since she stole away inside the dumpster. As nasty as the quarters were, Roxie didn't dare peek out of it until the sun went down. She dug in her bag to see what munchies she could scrounge together before she was desperate enough to go dumpster diving.

Roxie never noticed the shadow lengthening along the back of the dumpster. The hand reached into the dumpster dragging a rag across her mouth and nose. As she struggled against the increasing pressure, she let loose the urine she worked so hard to keep inside for the past few hours.

The shadow figure pulled Roxie out of the dumpster and dumped her into the back seat of the Buick LeSabre. The gloved hand snapped the plastic ties in place around her ankles and put another around her wrists before slapping duct tape over her mouth. The driver looked around to make certain they weren't seen. After fastening the seatbelt, the driver slid into the driver's seat and slowly pulled off down the alleyway.

"You thought you were so slick. You didn't see or hear me. Well you aren't so slick now!"

The driver of the dark vehicle drove through the streets of Bel Air at a leisurely pace in order to avoid suspicion. The interior of the car was spotless and smelled of violets. The driver wore creased pants, shined shoes, an all-weather coat, and driving gloves.

The driver pulled up to a secluded property off Jarrettsville Road and followed the long drive up to the main house.

The driver maneuvered the car into the detached garage and turned off the engine. Quickly closing the garage door, the driver opened the rear passenger door, and reached for Roxie. Feeling for a pulse, the driver exhaled after feeling a strong pulse. The driver lifted Roxie out of the car and walked to a side door that led to the mud room of the home.

The home was immaculate and orderly except for the cot placed in the hallway off the main entrance. Roxie was unceremoniously dumped on the cot as her hands and feet were secured to the legs of the cot. A quilt was placed over her, and the lights dimmed in the hall and living room.

"You stay here. I will be back," the anonymous figure said. The driver walked back to the garage and started the vehicle.

Roxie dreamed she was sitting in a dumpster. As she began to make her way to consciousness, she realized it was not a dream at all. She remembered being snatched out of that dumpster but couldn't recall anything else.

She began to cough as the effects of the drugs wore off, but she couldn't move her hands to cover her mouth.

Roxie had been in some trouble when she was a preteen but had pretty much straightened her life out after winding up in Ms. Cumbersome's foster care. Thanks to her friendship with Jenna, she knew life could be better if she did the right things.

This latest incident wasn't her fault. She must have seen something she shouldn't have or been in the wrong place at the wrong time.

Roxie was trying not to panic although her hands and feet were bound to whatever she was lying on. She listened for sounds of the person who brought her here but didn't hear anything. As she struggled against the ropes, the cot gave way and hit the ground hard, pinning her hands underneath.

"Owww!" yelled Roxie, "Somebody help me," she screamed.

"What have you done to yourself?" The voice said.

Roxie began to cry as she wondered if she would truly die tonight of the pain in her hands or at the mercy of the mystery person.

At once Roxie was sat up straight, the restraints were cut, and her hands freed. Two hands lifted her up in the air and placed her on a soft surface.

"Thank you. Look I don't know what's going on, and I don't care. I haven't seen your face, and I just want to get out of here. I won't call the cops or anything. Please let me go."

"You are safe here. I'm just going to restrain your hands and feet. I don't want you to hurt yourself trying to get away again."

"I wasn't trying to get away," Roxie said. "The thing gave away, and it fell. Please believe me. I don't know what this is about. Just let me go."

"As I've said, you are safe here. You are only being restrained to keep you from hurting yourself."

The voice sounded familiar, but Roxie couldn't tell if it belonged to a man or woman.

"Do I know you?"

"We have never met. I saved you from yourself and brought you here. You were in a lot of trouble; I'm helping you stay out of trouble. Believe me; you are better off with me than the person who was trying to snatch you before I got there."

The voice placed a glass against Roxie's lips and urged her to drink. The cool water slid down her throat and quenched her thirst. Roxie slowly began to drift off to sleep. It was going to be a lot better than the reality she was leaving behind. The figure smoothed Roxie's hair down and pulled the quilt higher around her shoulders.

The voice walked over to the radio in the corner of the room and turned on a classical music station. After a few moments, the deep, dark sounds of a bassoon filled the room. The voice sat in a darkened corner playing the song on the radio from memory. After accompanying several more songs, the voice cleaned the instrument and stored it back in the case.

Roxie could hear what sounded like heavenly music to her ears and wondered if she had died and gone to heaven. As the fog lifted from her brain, she raised her head and tried to talk to God.

"I'm sorry for all that I've done. I know I haven't been a good person. I've tried, but I always make a mess of things. Please, please forgive me. I don't know if it's too late, but I don't want to go to hell."

Roxie cried as she remembered all the stories Jenna told her about heaven and hell.

"Why are you thinking about dying, when you have so much to live for, young lady," said the voice. "I didn't save you in order to kill you."

"Then why am I here? Why are you holding me here if you are not trying to do nothing?"

"As I've told you, I rescued you from that gentleman in the alley. I've brought you here to rest and to keep you safe. No one is going to find you here. I need time to figure out what you've gotten yourself into."

"Well if you not going to kill me can I have a drink and some food please?"

The voice got up from the seat and entered the kitchen. Roxie could hear the sounds of pots and pans. After a few minutes, she could smell the spices and hear the sound of meat frying.

The torturous preparations yielded a meal for royalty. Strong hands placed in her mouth the sweetest tasting fried chicken Roxie had ever eaten.

The next bite was of crisp green beans flavored with smoked meat. Roxie wished the hand would feed her faster or release her hands so she could feed herself.

"I see you're impatient my dear. You must learn to wait on the things meant for you, and once you obtain it, savor it. You rush through everything without thinking and often miss the lesson. If you miss the lesson, you will have to repeat it. Unfortunately, you've repeated too many lessons and wasted a lot of time."

"How do you know what I've done and what's happened to me? You don't know me. You say we haven't met before, but you act like you know everything about me."

"I didn't say I didn't know you. In actuality, I know quite a bit about little Ms. Roxie Vega. You are wasting time when you could eat instead."

The voice continued to spoon feed Roxie until she was full. Struggling against sleep, Roxie's head began to nod as she fought to stay awake.

"Go to sleep Ms. Vega. All will be well. No harm will come to you here."

"I don't want to die. I'm not going to try to escape..." Roxie's voice drifted off until the soft sounds of her gentle breaths filled the space.

"You will need your rest as we have much to do tomorrow."

The voice laid Roxie down on the couch and covered her with a blanket. The voice sat in the corner of the room, opened the dusty case, and withdrew the bassoon. As the music played softly, the night deepened, and the shadows lengthened while Roxie rested nearby.

CHAPTER 6

Stan was nervous. He paced the tile floor. All Stan cared about was Kendra's health. He had never been so scared in his life. The sight of Kendra passed out on the bathroom floor removed all sexual thoughts from his mind.

"I hope she is okay," Stan whispered as he sat in the hard plastic seat in the waiting room. Stan glanced around the waiting room. He wondered if anyone from work was planning to stop by. It didn't matter to him because he was here for his Kendra.

"Family of Kendra Walker, please come to the nurses' station," paged the head nurse. Stan picked up his hat and made his way toward the nurses' station.

"I'm Kendra Walker's family. How is she doing?"

"Sir, she is in room 136, straight down the hall."

"Thank you, Miss." Stan closed the distance between him and the door to room 136. He held his hat in his hand and pushed the door open but quickly grabbed the handle.

Kendra would appreciate me knocking on the door, Stan thought as he gently knocked on the door. He didn't get a response and slowly opened the door.

As he stuck his head in the door, he could hear soft whimpers coming from the bed.

"Hey Kendra, it's me, Stan. Are you okay?"

Kendra slowly removed the covers from over her head and stared up at Stan with one of the saddest looks he ever saw. Stan didn't hesitate to walk over to the bed and gently picked up her hand.

"I don't know what is going on Kendra, but I'm willing to do whatever it takes to fix it."

"No one can fix it, Stan." Kendra withdrew her hand from Stan's. "I'm just so tired and want to be left alone."

Kendra turned her back and pulled the covers over her head. As she adjusted the covers, Stan saw her hair slide back to reveal a clean shaven head. He realized then that Kendra was bald under her hair weave.

Gently, Stan laid his hand on her shoulder. "I know you said you wanted to be alone, but I'm here for you. I don't know what you are going through…"

"You are right; you don't know what I'm going through. All you see is a chance to try to get in my pants, Stan. I know you watch me all of the time and probably fantasize about me. But you don't know the real me. No one does." Kendra sniffed as she stared at the wall. Soft sobs escaped from her lips.

Stan sat and listened to Kendra's sobs. He realized he didn't know much about Kendra other than her beautiful appearance. He began to wonder what was going on with her, how her hair fell out, and whether she had some kind of terminal illness.

"Kendra, if you don't mind, I would like to call someone for you. Is your family in this area? I really don't want to leave you here alone."

Kendra sat up in the bed and looked Stan in the eye. "I don't have any family. Here or otherwise. I'm all alone and have been most of my life. I can handle myself. I appreciate you coming with me, but I would rather you leave."

"Okay. I understand," Stan said as he wrote down his cell phone number and handed it to Kendra. "If you need me, please call."

Stan picked up his hat and walked out of Kendra's room. As he made his way toward the bank of elevators, he wondered who Kendra Walker really was and how he could help her.

Stan waited for the elevator, and overheard someone nearby talking.

"I'm at the hospital. Yeah I know the job was botched. I can't do nothing about it. They said those two people are here somewhere but won't release any info on them. Do you still got that chick we snatched?"

Stan thought they were talking about his coworkers. He glanced down the long tiled hallway but didn't see anyone. He was hesitant to get involved but realized it may have something to do with Kendra.

He inched his way around the corner and saw a tall, older, white gentleman, talking on a cell phone in front of some vending machines. Stan reached in his pocket and prayed for some change. He located a dollar bill and walked toward the snack machine. The man turned, closed his cell phone, and walked toward Stan.

Stan couldn't make out his features because of the fedora covering his eyes. But he did notice the man was clean shaven, had a long scar on the left side of his face, and was over six feet tall.

"Hey man, you got change for a dollar?" Stan asked as the gentleman walked past him.

"No, I don't have any change. Sorry buddy."

The gentleman walked toward the elevators. Stan walked a few steps behind. The elevator's timely arrival allowed Stan to enter right behind the gentleman.

When the elevator reached the lobby filled with patients, staff, and visitors, the tall gentleman walked in the opposite direction of the parking lot. Stan stayed behind him and followed him toward a stairwell exit.

The man turned sharply into a non-marked door that led to a loading dock at the rear of the hospital. The gentleman's quick steps clicked along the loading dock, down a short flight of steps, and into a waiting limousine. The license plate was partially blocked by a stack of linen, but Stan was able to write down XG451.

Stan watched as the limousine headed to Route 24 toward Forest Hill and Jarrettsville.

"What is going on around here?" Stan murmured as he made his way toward the parking garage.

Kendra looked out the private room window at the parking garage below and wondered if Stan was coming back. She didn't lie to Stan when she told him she had no family or friends to speak of.

Kendra grew up in a home with a bipolar mother and a father who lived in denial. Her fondest memories of her childhood are also some of the worst memories.

One time in particular, Kate, Kendra's mom, baked chocolate chip cookies, Kendra's favorite, for her school fundraiser. Kate hadn't taken her medication as ordered because she was trying to self-medicate with herbal medicines in an effort to gain some control.

Kate came to Johnnycake Elementary school with the baked goods and was directed to the gymnasium where several classes were setting up tables. Kendra's mom was so pretty dressed in her Donna Karan sheath dress and her hair in an up-do; she looked like a mom out of a Macy's sales ad.

Kendra's mom slammed the cookies on one table causing two others filled with baked goods to slide onto the gym floor as Kendra watched in horror.

Her mom attempted to pick them up but became more agitated and began to moan and rock. Kendra ran over, wrapped her arms around her and quietly whispered calming words in her ears. She helped her mom up from the floor and could hear the chatter.

"I wonder what's wrong with her mom?"

"Is her mom crazy or what?"

"That poor little girl. I wonder where her father is and if he knows what is going on?"

Kendra walked her mom to the car, but refused to cry as she listened to the unkind words spoken in her hearing. She put her mother in the driver's seat and walked around to the passenger door. She was tempted to look back at the school. Fifteen minutes later, her mom started the car for home as if nothing had happened.

Four years later, during Kendra's last year of middle school, her mom was committed to a mental institution. Kendra's dad left shortly thereafter but maintained the household expenses.

Kendra kept the pretense that someone was home in order to keep from being sent to a foster home. Kendra raised herself by learning to write checks, contact maintenance companies, and prepare her own meals. She also made her hair and doctor appointments.

Kendra excelled in school despite the strange circumstances and received a full scholarship to the University of Maryland Eastern Shore. Her father continued to provide monthly checks until her final year of college.

Although she hadn't seen him in years, Kendra knew he still cared for her. Each year she received a birthday card and a Christmas present.

Kate died of natural causes two years ago, and Kendra attended the funeral alone. Her father paid for the burial but did not attend the service.

Kendra was finally free to live the life she had dreamed of but wasn't sure what the dream was anymore. What her colleagues didn't understand was Kendra always had to act older, be more mature than her peers. She wasn't allowed to get wild or be a normal teenager. She spent too much time covering up the fact that she had no one to guide her.

Gertrude tried to befriend Kendra and mentor her, but she shunned the attention. Kendra was uncomfortable around Gertrude because she often asked the hard questions that others thought but often didn't voice. One time after a HR staff meeting, Gertrude walked up to Kendra and asked her to attend a get-together at her home and told her to feel free to bring a guest.

"Listen honey, as cute as you are, you've got to have someone special somewhere," said Gertrude.

"I don't have anyone that I'm seeing regularly. I'm dating several men and don't see a need to bring them around people I know," Kendra blurted out without a thought.

"Oh, is that right?" Gertrude raised her eyebrow and appeared to look into Kendra's soul. "Well I can certainly understand that. You just never know when one of them will turn into a stalker or worse, a serious contender."

Kendra turned and walked down the hall. She didn't understand some of the things Gertrude said, but she always felt exposed when the conversation was over. That was the reason she didn't let herself get close to people. She wasn't good in social situations and often felt intimidated by men.

Although the office gossip had her pegged as a gold-digger, Kendra in fact was still a virgin. She was horrified of the thought of revealing herself to a man in that way. Her mother left before she could explain human sexuality, and the information Kendra received in school and on the playground filled her with in irrational fear of the very act.

Kendra loved sexy clothes, which she didn't wear growing up. As an adult, she loved the way she looked in the mirror and appreciated the attention, which affirmed her existence in a way nothing else did.

The other reason she wasn't intimate was because Kendra knew a man would want to know why she was bald.

During one of her mother's bad days, Kate called Kendra into the bathroom after complaining about her "beady bead" hair. The thick hair was matted to Kendra's scalp from lack of attention.

Kate cut all of Kendra's beautiful hair off and put Nair hair remover on her scalp. The product burned out the roots and hair never grew back in its place. When Kate realized what she had done, she began to purchase wigs for Kendra to wear. Kendra never learned to swim because she was afraid her wig would come off. When she got older, she was able to afford custom-made wigs for chemotherapy patients.

Kendra heard a knock at the door as the tears began to dry on her face. "Come in." Kendra turned toward the door and was astonished to see Stan in the doorway holding flowers in one hand and a bag of great smelling food in another.

"I called, and they told me you could have soup and other bland food. No grease or heavy food," Stan said.

He smiled at Kendra as he walked into the room. He laid the food on the table in the corner and turned back toward Kendra.

"Stan, I don't know what to say. No one has ever done anything nice for me or cared for me before. You don't even know me."

"Kendra, I owe you an apology. You are right. I don't know you and assumed false things about you. Please give me a chance to get to know you as a friend."

Stan watched Kendra's face spread into a small smile. He realized for the first time in his life, he actually cared about a woman's feelings.

"Did you want to eat your wonton soup in bed or at the table?"

"I feel okay. I will sit at the table."

Stan helped seat Kendra at the small table. He pulled the hot soup out of the paper bag, and handed Kendra a spoon. He also gave her a can of ginger ale and some napkins.

"What are you going to eat?"

"The wontons out of your soup. You can't have those," Stan said. He pulled a spoon out of his inside jacket pocket and scooped a fat wonton out of the container.

Kendra relaxed and began to sip the soup as Stan recounted the adventure involving the strange man in the limousine. A half hour later, a nurse entered the room to take Kendra's vital signs. Kendra made her way over to the bed and allowed the nurse to poke and prod her for a few minutes.

"The doctor should be here in a few minutes to speak to you," the nurse said on her way out of the room.

"Did you want me to stay until you find out what is going on?"

Kendra shook her head yes, and Stan settled into his chair. "Do you want to watch some TV until he gets here or keep chatting?"

"Turn to the news; let's see if there's any update on our coworkers."

"I don't want you to be upset. You've had a long day and should get some rest. The TV may only raise your blood pressure or something."

"I appreciate your concern, but I am a grown woman," Kendra said a little more forcefully than she meant but wanted Stan to understand she was in control.

"How about channel 15?"

"That works. I'm sorry; it's just that I've been on my own for most of my life and I don't like feeling out of control. Thank you for coming back. I know you didn't have to do that, and I appreciate it."

"I want to be here for you Kendra not because I want something from you but because I care. I do admit at first, I just wanted to be with you because I thought… well, you know…"

"You thought you could get in my pants. I know what you and all of the men in that office say about me. It's not true. I'm not a gold-digger or a loose woman."

"I know, Kendra. I'm sorry. But I'm here, and I do want to get to know more about you if you will let me in. No pressure, just as friends."

Stan hoped she would understand he meant every word. He wanted to be in her presence and would do whatever it took just to be there.

Down the hall, one woman regretted the choice she made to be with a man at all cost. Madeline Shaw could not believe how one bad decision led to so many more. She now understood the saying beat within an inch of her life. One more inch to the right and she would have been downstairs in the morgue. She suffered a concussion, a dislocated shoulder, and bruises that covered her body from head to toe. Madeline was in so much pain it hurt to think. How it came to this, she wouldn't be able to explain to anyone. She closed her eyes as tears fell like large salt drops from her eyes.

Madeline remembered the day she fell in love with Worrell Stevens. It was at the office monthly birthday celebration. She stood in line waiting for a slice of the red velvet cake when he walked up to her and brushed too close.

"I'm sorry." Worrell leaned in close and spoke so softly it felt like a caress.

"That's okay. It's kind of tight in here with all of the extra chairs."

Madeline pulled her neck scarf tighter around her neck in an effort to cover the bruises.

She watched him from her hooded eyelids as he chatted with his coworkers. Madeline wanted to go sit next to him but figured that would be too obvious. She knew she'd find a way to get him to notice her.

Madeline pressed the call button in hopes the nurse would return shortly. The pain medicine wore off almost half an hour ago and she needed something now.

"Ms. Shaw, I'm sorry to keep you waiting. What can I help you with?" the nurse said.

Madeline lifted her arm and pointed towards the IV bag. Unfortunately, she couldn't speak and only managed to make gurgling sounds. She prayed the nurse understood.

"You need something for the pain? I'll be right back." The nurse turned and walked out of the room.

Madeline's eyes fluttered closed as the pain overtook her consciousness. By the time the nurse returned, Madeline had fallen asleep. Her last conscious thought was centered on Worrell and if he fared any better than she did.

Worrell tried to sit up but the pain inside his head made him lie still. He could feel his toes move and was glad for the feeling. He was worried that the blow to his head and neck rendered him paralyzed.

The last thing he remembered right before he was hit, was walking into Madeline's office to ask a question.

What he saw he couldn't believe. Madeline was sitting in her chair with a long band tied around her throat and attached to her ankles.

"What are you doing?" he said as he rushed towards Madeline. His world went black before he could reach her.

CHAPTER 7

Chuck Tobias knew his days were numbered. He had been slacking off at work for the last six months and knew that someone was auditing his work. He didn't know who or why, but he felt it. As he gathered the applications, which the detectives finally released to him, he couldn't help but feel like this whole situation was a set up.

This morning Rachel date-stamped the applications with yesterday's date. Human Resources did not take a day off even if two of its employees were severely injured and one was missing. It amazed him that the senior level officers were more concerned with filling vacant positions than the previous day's events.

"They will walk over my dead, cold body and replace me with a younger, more technologically savvy specialist," Chuck murmured as he glanced over the applications.

He dialed Rachel's extension but got her voicemail. "Rachel, this is Chuck. When you get a moment, please bring me the Public Information Specialist and Human Resource Officer folders. Thanks."

There were over forty-five applications received yesterday for the Public Information Specialist position. The Human Resource Officer position had well over three times that amount. With a starting salary of over one hundred thousand dollars, it attracted quite a number of highly qualified individuals.

"It will be interesting to see what demon gets promoted up in here," Chuck said under his breath.

"I prefer an angel myself," said Rachel, laughing as she entered Chuck's office. "I'm praying for divine intervention and the removal of all demons, present company excluded."

"Laugh all you want, Rachel. I'm telling you this place has gone to hell. We've got missing coworkers, poisoned ones, and two beat up managers."

"Wait a minute. Who was poisoned?"

"I didn't say anything about poison. What are you talking about? You were so busy praising the Lord, you weren't listening to me."

"No, I distinctly heard you say we've got missing coworkers, poisoned ones, and two beat up managers. As far as we know we've only got one missing coworker and two beat up managers."

"It's been a hell of a long day and night. I'm about delirious looking at these applications. So I'm inaccurate, sue me."

"Whatever, Chuck. Just make sure you review these applications closely. The last vacancy announcement, you referred two unqualified individuals and denied applications for six highly qualified applicants. We had two grievances, which we had to settle because of it."

"How about you worry about doing your job and let me do my job. It was an honest mistake."

"Okay," Rachel said. She shook her head as she walked out of his office and down the hallway toward her cubicle.

Rachel continued to date-stamp applications and filed them into the appropriate folder. In the middle of the pile was a folded letter. Rachel began to read and screamed in horror at the words on the page.

We have Helena Perkins. Do what we say, and she won't get hurt. Have her fiancé bring two million dollars to the lighthouse in Havre de Grace at 10 pm tomorrow. No cops.

Rachel dialed the local police as a crowd began to gather around her desk. She looked around for Gertrude and wondered where she was, but her missive was cut short by the dispatcher on the other line.

"Bel Air Police," the dispatcher said curtly.

"This is Rachel Ward, and I'm calling from the Human Resources office located on Hickory Avenue. We received a ransom note for Helena Perkins, our missing coworker."

"Please do not allow anyone else to touch that piece of paper or anything else with it. We are sending a detective over."

"Thanks ma'am." Her hands shook as she ended the call. She quoted Psalm 91 in order to get God's peace to fall over her. She couldn't do it on her own. As she prayed for protection for Helena, the peace that surpasses all understanding enveloped her, and she calmed down.

"Okay people, what is going on here?" asked Miguel, who walked into the suite. "I heard screams out in the lobby near the men's room."

"Miguel, we received a ransom note for Helena."

"Let me see it mija." Miguel reached toward Rachel, extending his hand.

Rachel snatched it away from Miguel and placed the note in her lower drawer.

"The police told me not to let anyone else touch it. They are on their way over."

The mention of police seemed to break up the nosy crowd. Rachel could not believe how the office seemed to run in spite of the events of the last twenty-four hours. People were standing around chit-chatting, drinking coffee, and talking about the last American Idol show results.

"This is complete madness," Rachel uttered as she sat at her desk waiting for the police to arrive.

"Rachel, madness doesn't begin to describe what is going on."

Rachel looked up into Denise's serious face.

"There is some serious warfare going on in this place. I don't know why, but I sense not only the presence of evil but also the warring angels of God. I think we need to fast and pray this week to take back this building."

Rachel's mouth dropped open as she listened to Denise talk about spiritual warfare. Denise rarely talked to anyone, but for her to break out in conversation about spiritual things reminded Rachel that God was still in control.

"That's a good idea Denise. We need to be prayerful about what is going on around here. We've got that HR Officer posting that just closed, and we want to make certain we get a godly individual in this place. We didn't pray the last time and received a second level demon."

"I've been praying about the strange information I found in one of my reports. I'm not sure what it all means yet, but I'm hoping God will reveal it to me."

Before Rachel could determine what the strange information was, Denise disappeared. The ringing telephone took her attention and she soon forgot about Denise and Chuck's strange comments.

Fifteen minutes after placing the call to the police, Detective Gentry and another detective arrived. Rachel quickly reviewed what occurred and how she discovered the note. She opened her drawer and watched as Detective Gentry retrieved the note with his gloved hand and placed the note in a plastic bag.

"Ms. Ward, I'm Detective Betancourt. What can you tell me about Helena Perkins?"

"Ms. Perkins is one of our Recruitment and Placement Specialists. She is engaged to Taurean Harris, a former NFL player. They are supposed to get married in a few months."

"Do you know of any reason why someone would kidnap her?"

"I know of about a million reasons," Rachel said as she rolled her eyes at Detective Betancourt's question. "Her fiancé is worth millions. Isn't that reason enough?"

"Well actually Mrs. Ward, her fiancé is in fact quite broke. So the kidnappers are under the same false impression as everyone else in this office."

Rachel decided she didn't like Detective Betancourt very much. There was a way to do certain things, and she handled this case very wrong.

"Is there anything else I can help you with Detective Betancourt?"

"There is one other thing. What can you tell me about the relationship between Gertrude Judkins and Officer Jax Washington?"

"Who is Jax Washington, and what does he have to do with Gertrude?"

"Officer Washington was on duty here yesterday morning when your office opened. It appears he has taken a shine to Ms. Judkins and has escorted her to the hospital to see her injured daughter as well as brought Ms. Judkins to the police station for questioning."

"Jenna was injured? What is going on?"

"Why do you find it your business to tell my business?" Gertrude stated firmly as she walked toward Rachel. "You act more like a jealous woman than a professional in search of clues. I would think you would spend more time trying to figure out what you get paid to do and leave me and my relationships alone. Rachel, I need to see you in my office."

Gertrude briskly walked down the office hallway with Rachel pulling up the rear.

"Gertrude, what the heck is going on? Who is Officer Washington? Better yet, what is wrong with my niece? She isn't trying out for another athletic team is she?"

"We need to pray, and then I will tell you everything. If I don't pray, I'm going to march down that hall and snatch that dwarf with all the mouth out of her cheap shoes!"

"Well Gertrude, if you don't, I will!"

They laughed, then quickly sobered and prayed for the circumstances. Gertrude prayed aloud for Jenna, Helena, Madeline, and Worrell. Silently, Gertrude prayed for Washington and the strength to keep from choking him after he left her at the station with that detective.

After a few moments of intense prayer, Gertrude released Rachel's hands and directed her to a seat.

"You need to stay off your feet and put them up. Your ankles are a little swollen."

"Who is Washington, and why does that detective think you guys are too friendly? But before you answer that, please tell me about Jenna."

"My daughter decided to submit her application to our office right before midnight and took a blow to the head. She's okay but fractured her wrist apparently in the fall."

"Oh Gertrude, I'm so sorry and glad it wasn't too serious. I know this has shaken you up."

"Definitely, I thought she was having a clumsy moment. I get to the hospital and Darius is explaining…"

"How is Mr. Sexy Ex? How are you doing after being in his presence?"

"Well I managed to keep down last night's dinner, if that's what you mean. Seriously though, it went okay. The man grates my nerves with his doggish ways. Do you know that fool was macking out some woman and then tried to act like I was his wife when she turned stalker!"

Rachel shook her head as she watched her friend try to process Darius's latest stunt. Over the years her friend had tried to get over Darius with various levels of success. It seemed just when she was over Darius, he would reel her back in, and Rachel would have to deprogram her friend.

Gertrude explained it years ago. Darius was the first man she loved after playing the field for most of her adult life. He was smooth, fine, and seemed to be all into Gertrude. Unfortunately, his attention span was short lived.

Rachel never thought they were a good match. From everything Gertrude had told her and she was able to put together, they were as different as a Jaguar and a Pinto. But sometimes extreme differences work in a relationship.

Lately Gertrude hadn't dated much. She seemed to wall herself off and take pleasure in torturing her friends with her horrible cooking and even worse baking disasters.

Rachel remembered the time Gertrude offered to bake an egg and sausage pastry ring for the office. It was a beautiful sight to see, but when Chuck cut the first slice, runny eggs and raw dough ran from the seam. Rachel encouraged her coworkers to cut a slice, put it on a small plate, and toss the plate in the nearest trashcan. That turned out to be a big mistake because Gertrude brought one to every breakfast meeting. That is until Chuck convinced the HR officer to only allow afternoon potlucks.

"Rachel, are you listening to me? I was trying to tell you about Judas, posing as a police officer."

Rachel looked up into Gertrude's fiery eyes and realized that she was serious. "Gertrude, I thought the cop's name was Jax something-or-other."

"His name is Jackson Washington. What kind of person has two last names? I should not have trusted that caramel kiss."

"What are you mumbling about? He kissed you?"

"No Rachel, he betrayed me without the kiss. I cannot believe I fell for the okeydoke-knight-in-shining-armor."

"Focus Gertrude; start at the beginning."

Gertrude began to retell the tale of the previous day's adventure while Rachel watched the range of emotions on her friend's face. One thing about Gertrude—you could tell by looking at her what she was feeling or thinking. As a negotiator, she knew her stuff, but her poker face needed some work.

"I'm telling you that man wrecked my gall. I was so upset with him but more upset with myself for trusting someone that soon. Just because he had the sexiest lips known to man and treated me like the 90 pound woman trapped inside of me, does not mean I should have let my guard down."

"I didn't realize you thought my lips were sexy," Jax Washington said as he held open Gertrude's door.

Rachel turned to face the voice and grinned as she watched the interplay between the two. She could immediately tell why Gertrude was so steamed. This tall man was sexy and fine.

"Who let you in this building, Officer Washington? I thought I told you I didn't want to see you again?"

"No, you didn't say that. What you actually said was, and I quote, 'I thought you were trying to help me not deliver me like some kind of Judas.' Am I right?"

Rachel turned her head quickly from Officer Washington back to Gertrude. Gertrude's normally cool exterior was replaced with flared nostrils, fiery eyes, and tight lips. That was Rachel's cue to exit.

"I've got work to do. I'm Rachel Ward, Gertrude's friend and coworker. If you need inside information on handling her, please let me know. I will talk to you later Gertrude," Rachel said as she quickly eased her way out of the door.

"Rachel, I can't stand you right now." Gertrude gritted her teeth and rolled her eyes at Rachel.

"I apologize for Gertrude's rudeness. I know she is normally a kind, sensitive woman, but she is mad at me and took it out on you," Jax said. He closed the door and turned his full attention to Gertrude.

Gertrude couldn't help but admire Jax's appearance. Once again he exuded pure testosterone in his black-on-black jeans and jacket. His signature scent was wreaking havoc with her senses, but she was determined to remain focused and thoroughly pissed.

"You've got a lot of nerve coming here, Officer Washington."

"Gertrude, let me tell you up front that I don't believe in moving backwards but always forwards."

"What does that mean?"

"It means we have already established a first name basis, and I'm not going back to formalities. Now I can appreciate you are a little teed off at me, but I want to explain."

Jax didn't wait for Gertrude's permission but settled in his chair, crossed his legs and stated his case.

"I know it looks bad. I did volunteer to pick you up, but you've got to know I didn't know Betancourt was going to do all of that. I didn't know she was even assigned to this case."

"Jax, I was humiliated, alone, and in need of assistance. You left me there to face her and her alternate agenda. I don't know what's happened between you two, but leave me out of your little tête-à-tête."

"Gertrude, I don't have to explain anything to you because we haven't agreed to be exclusive, but I haven't dated Detective Betancourt. She would like to make me her man, but so far, I've successfully dodged that bullet. I didn't leave you, I was ordered out. I would never leave you unprotected, please believe me."

Gertrude stopped listening to his explanation after she heard the word exclusive, which implied dating, when they weren't even dating!

"Jax, how should I put this? We are not dating, and we will never date!"

"You are cute when you are agitated. I like the whole nostril flaring bit." Jax stood up and walked around to Gertrude's side of the table. He offered his hand to her, and as she extended her hand, he gently tugged her to her feet.

"I need you to look me in my eyes while I tell you I apologize for leaving you behind. I only wanted to protect you and only caused you pain. Do you forgive me?"

As Gertrude looked into his big brown eyes, she realized she wanted Jax to protect her for a very long time. Gertrude shook her head to rid herself of the thought.

She playfully pushed against his chest and sat back in her chair.

"You are not getting off that easy Mr. Man."

Jax smiled as he realized they turned the corner in their budding friendship.

"That's why I packed a picnic lunch for you. It is waiting in the back of my truck."

Jax held out his hand and prayed Gertrude would accept his invitation to lunch. Gertrude placed her hand in his and Jax thought life couldn't get any better than this.

Gertrude grabbed her bag as her cell phone began to chime. "That's Darius, my ex-husband. He may be calling about Jenna," she said as she flipped her phone open.

"Gert, they just released our baby girl. I'm going to take her home."

"Does she have her key so you can get in?"

"I'm taking her home to my house. She doesn't need to be alone in your house especially since we don't know who did this or why."

"Let me talk to her."

"Hi Mom, Dad's taking me to his house. I will chat at you later because we are getting on the elevator."

"Gert, I've got this. I will call you once we get to the house."

"Bye Darius."

Jax took a long look at Gertrude while she spoke on the phone. Her normally straight back seemed to hunch a little while she spoke to her ex-husband. But her countenance brightened when she looked at Jax and rewarded him with that million dollar smile of hers.

"Is everything all right with your daughter?"

"Yes. Darius is going to take her to his house."

"That's good. She shouldn't be alone until we know what is going on." Jax escorted Gertrude through the office and deflected the stares he received.

He walked Gertrude around the side of the building toward his truck. He pulled open the tailgate and took down the bistro table and two chairs.

Gertrude stood back and watched in amazement as Jax transformed the space into an outdoor restaurant. He placed a purple tablecloth on top of the table and laid out purple and white plates with matching cups. He had a vase of purple flowers in the middle.

"How did you know purple was my favorite color?"

"I didn't. When I saw it in the store it reminded me of you."

Jax set several steaming cartons of delicious smelling food in front of them. He opened the cartons to reveal several different dishes of Chinese, Mexican, and Jamaican food.

"I wasn't sure what type of food you liked, so I figured I better get everything. This is shrimp with garlic sauce, the other is black beans and roast pork, and the last is curried chicken. There is a carton of fried rice and one of white rice."

"Jax, this is wonderful, and I love all of them."

Jax picked up Gertrude's plate and placed a little of each on her plate and set it in front of her. He repeated the process with his own. He set out bottles of sweet tea and lemon packets.

"Give me your hand so I can say grace." Jax stretched out his hand expectantly toward Gertrude.

"Father, I thank you for second chances, beautiful company, and the wonderful food prepared by others. Use this food for nourishment, bless the hands that prepared it and let this be the beginning of something wonderful. It's in your Son's name I pray, amen."

They silently ate their meal, pausing to look up at one another as the sun beamed down on their faces.

"Jax, this was wonderful, and I truly enjoyed your company. I've got a ton of work to do, so I must get back in the office."

"I hope you forgive me. Let me clean up, and I will walk you back into the building."

"Jax, that's not necessary. I've been walking unaccompanied into the building for a long time now."

Gertrude placed her napkin on the table and stood up. Jax placed his hand on her elbow and drew her close to him. He leaned his clean shaven face down into her ear and whispered, "I apologize to you in advance for what I'm going to do."

Jax turned Gertrude around and placed the gentlest kiss she'd ever felt on her lips. He took her by the elbow and walked her to the front of the building as the shock of what happened settled in.

"I'll look forward to your call later. Be good Gertrude."

Jax spun around and headed for his truck. He quickly cleaned off the table and put everything back into the truck. He sat in the front seat and waited a few moments to see if Gertrude was going to come back out. He was disappointed and relieved at the same time.

Jax couldn't believe he shut Gertrude up but really looked forward to the tongue lashing he knew he would receive later. A slow, sexy grin made its way across his face as he pulled out of the parking lot and headed toward home.

Detective Betancourt was standing on the loading dock smoking a cigarette as she watched Officer Washington pull out of the parking lot. She stomped on her cigarette butt, grimaced, and spit a wad of gum off the loading dock.

Gertrude sat at her desk in a daze. She looked out her office window at the public parking garage across the street. The sunlight struck the security cameras, which gave the appearance of twinkling stars.

"That's it. The security cameras should show what happened the other night." Gertrude jumped up from her desk and ran out her office door.

"Where's Detective Betancourt?" Gertrude yelled as she made her way down the hall.

"I was just on my way to see you, Ms. Judkins," Detective Betancourt snarled. "I didn't want to disturb your cozy moment with Officer Washington."

Gertrude looked down at Detective Betancourt, counted to ten and then fifteen before she spoke.

"Detective, did you pull the tapes from the cameras in the parking garage across the street?"

"Why are you questioning me about cameras? Are you worried the cameras will show you have something to do with what happened? Or are you more worried that your boyfriend will be guilty of something?

Gertrude spun on her heels and headed back to her office. As she continued to try her "woo saw" methods to calm her pressure, Rachel walked into her office.

"I overheard what the little witch said. I'm sorry she keeps trying to get to you."

"It's okay. Who do we know over at the Sheriff's office? I need someone to pull those security camera tapes from the parking garage. Or at least give me some unofficial information on what's on them."

"What about the husband and wife team from your church, John and Nettie?"

"Good idea Rachel. I have John's cell phone. Here's the number; see what you can find out. If Detective Betancourt wants to speak to me again, I'm unavailable."

"Gertrude, are you okay? Although you seem pissed at Detective Betancourt on the surface, you have this inner glow emanating off your skin. You are positively glowing."

"I tasted the caramel kiss, and I think I'm hooked."

Rachel grabbed the seat in front of Gertrude's desk, leaned on her elbows, and waited for the juicy details, "Spill it, girlfriend."

"He set up a bistro table, with Chinese, Mexican, and Jamaican food, all set on a purple tablecloth with purple flowers in a purple vase."

"Oh my, it seems Officer Washington isn't playing with you. What are you going to do about it?"

"I'm going to enjoy the ride as long as it lasts. I like Jax. He's interesting."

"I'm glad you've met a nice man Gertrude. I hope it continues. Switching gears, can you believe we received a ransom note for Helena and that crazy detective says Taurean is broke?"

"I wouldn't trust everything Betancourt says. Something about that woman isn't right."

"You aren't saying that because you are feeling Officer Washington are you?

"Rachel, how long have you known me?"

"Five long years. Why?"

"I can read people, and I'm telling you, something is off… In the meantime, try to get a hold of John and see what he knows about the security tapes."

"Aye-aye captain." She saluted and walked out of the office.

Gertrude turned to her computer and waited for her Outlook email to open up. Gertrude served as a labor/employee relations or LER specialist for the company. As an LER specialist, Gertrude spent the majority of her time acting as a management representative during labor disputes. The other half of her job seemed to focus on employee misconduct.

Gertrude spent a great deal of her day answering management officials' questions on the collective bargaining agreement. She would provide answers based on the agreement, policy, or law. Oftentime her responses did not help management in their efforts to "get" an employee.

Human resources employees were both loved and hated by the staff they represented. When the opinions supported the action of the officials, they were loved. If the opinions were in opposition to the action, then the HR employees were hated.

HR employees must have thick skins and forgiving hearts. The manager who hung up the phone today would call tomorrow and ask for assistance during an intense meeting with the union. The managers expected professional and knowledgeable LER specialists.

Gertrude quickly went through her emails, provided contract interpretations to expectant managers, sent out calendar invites to union officials for grievance meetings, and sent letters she reviewed to management officials.

She rubbed her eyes and stretched her long limbs under her desk. Looking around the room, Gertrude studied the various photos of Jenna. Her daughter's transformation over the years never ceased to amaze Gertrude. Every school year, Gertrude set out the year's photos of Jenna's latest attempt at athletics. Several photos captured crutches, bruises, and even a black eye.

Jenna was determined to letter in a sport. By the end of her senior year in high school, Gertrude convinced Jenna the debate team was actually a mental form of athleticism and Jenna earned her letter. Darius and Gertrude were relieved the child had finally given up.

A sudden knock on the door shook Gertrude from her trip down memory lane.

"Come in."

Sonya slowly opened the door and walked into Gertrude's office, "Do you mind if I come in for a minute? I want to ask you a question."

Gertrude noticed Sonya's unkempt appearance and the bags under her eyes, "What's going on Sonya?"

"I think someone is trying to set me up."

"Why? For what?"

Sonya reached into her pocket and pulled out a wadded cloth reeking of blood. "I found this under my desk when I got back from lunch. It wasn't there when I left for lunch."

"How do you know it wasn't there?"

"I keep my bottle…I mean my personal belongings under the desk toward the back and I would have noticed it when I reached for my um…things."

"So let me get this straight. You reached under your desk for your things and didn't notice a wadded up cloth. But when you got back from lunch it was under the desk?"

"Yes."

"How long were you gone to lunch and who did you tell you were leaving?"

"I told Miguel I was going to the Greene Turtle for lunch. He asked me to pick him up some sliders."

"Did anyone else know you were going to the restaurant?"

"No, just Miguel," Sonya said as she stared off into space. She appeared a little discombobulated.

"Sonya, you need to take this cloth back to your office and call Detective Betancourt. Tell her what you told me."

"But what if someone is setting me up? I cannot go to jail for something I didn't do. I didn't want to be a part of this."

Gertrude's eyebrows shot up at Sonya's last statement. As she paid closer attention, Sonya was more fidgety than normal and her nails were chewed down to the nubs.

"You didn't want to be a part of what? Sonya, what is going on around here? What do you know?"

Sonya shot to her feet, grabbed the cloth and scooted out of Gertrude's door. Gertrude quickly dialed the sheriff's office and put in a call to Detective Betancourt. She recounted the conversation with Sonya and hung up the phone.

Gertrude massaged her temples and took deep breaths. She opened the cold bottle of water on the edge of her desk and took a long swallow.

The day was getting stranger by the hour.

CHAPTER 8

Darius opened the bedroom door a crack and poked his head in the room. Jenna was out like a light. *I cannot believe all that has happened. If I still drank, I would get me a taste,* thought Darius.

He walked down the hallway toward the living room. In the ten years since his divorce, he was able to rebuild his life, settle down, and purchase a nice home. Sparsely furnished with masculine, dark wood, it was a neat home that reflected the owner's need for space.

Just as Darius got settled on the couch, his doorbell rang.

"Who is it?" he asked.

"Open the door."

Darius tried to place the voice but couldn't recall the owner of the masculine voice.

"I'm not opening the door until I know who it is." He regretted not spending the extra fifteen dollars on a peephole.

Darius reached over for the baseball bat in the corner of the foyer. He took a step back and to the side just in case the owner of the voice had a firearm.

"It's me, Roxie."

Darius snatched open the door to admit his daughter's best friend.

"Roxie quit playing around. Where've you been? Jenna's been asking for you."

"You don't have enough time for me to explain all that's happened in the last forty-eight hours."

"Well come on in. Jenna's in the guest room asleep. Did you want something to drink?" Darius asked as he walked to the refrigerator to retrieve a soda.

"No. I just wanted to come by and see Jenna. I stopped by her house but she wasn't there. I called her job and they said she was in the hospital. What's going on?"

"When was the last time you spoke to Jenna?"

"I saw her last week. I was supposed to come see her Friday night, but I got distracted."

"Jenna was attacked last night while at the HR office on Hickory."

Roxie gasped loudly as her eyes watered up. "Is she okay? Oh-my-gosh-I-cannot-believe-what-is-going-on!" Roxie blurted out said without taking a breath.

"Do you know any reason someone would try to hurt my Pooka?"

"Mr. Darius, I was chased, snatched by one guy, and rescued by another. The last guy told me I must have witnessed something, but I don't know what it could be."

"Hold on Roxie. Did you call the police?"

"No, I was dropped off by the guy who rescued me. He said he would be in touch when he found out anything."

"You led a perfect stranger or kidnapper to my front door? You've got to be kidding me, Roxie. Tell me you are not that gullible."

Darius shot to his feet, ran to the front door and looked out the door. He looked right and left down his street but didn't see anything out of the ordinary.

"Mr. Darius, you know I'm straight street. I had old dude drop me off two blocks from here. I wasn't followed."

"I'm going to call the police."

A pounding on the front door a few minutes later startled the two sitting in the kitchen.

"Who the hell is it?"

"It's Officer Robertson, sir."

"Roxie, don't you move. I want to know what is going on, and you are going to tell me everything from the beginning."

"I don't know much, but I will tell you everything."

Darius glared at Roxie as he turned to walk toward the front door. Officer Robertson was in civilian clothes and holding a small plastic bag.

"Hello Mr. Judkins. I forgot I had Jenna's phone when I left the hospital. I stopped at the bakery on the way here and picked up a few black bottom cupcakes to cheer her up."

"Come on in Teddy. I'm sure Jenna will appreciate the cupcakes when she wakes up."

"Who are you talking to Daddy?" Jenna slowly walked out of her bedroom.

"I'm talking to Teddy Robertson. He brought you something."

Teddy couldn't help but admire Jenna's beauty, apparent even when she was wearing a t-shirt and sweat pants.

"Teddy Robertson? Oh my, you look great!" Jenna yelled as she ran toward Teddy and wrapped her arms around him. "Oh my gosh. Dad was right. You are not "little" Teddy, anymore. How've you been?"

Teddy was still stuck on the hug and unable to form words. Darius noted his muteness and patted the man on the back to lead him toward the living room.

Whenever Teddy was in Jenna's presence, he couldn't breathe let alone hold a conversation. His heart squeezed in his chest.

"I've been good. I didn't realize I took your cell phone when I left the hospital," Teddy said as he held out the phone to Jenna.

"Thanks Teddy. What's in the bag?"

"I stopped by Herman's Bakery and picked you up a few black bottoms. I remember they were your favorite."

"Stopped by Herman's? Teddy that's way over by…" Darius realizing this was a private moment between Teddy and Jenna, turned and walked toward the kitchen where he left Roxie earlier.

"Roxie," Darius yelled upon realizing Roxie was no longer sitting in the kitchen. He looked toward the back door and saw it was not shut all the way. He didn't know what kind of trouble Roxie was in but prayed it didn't bring her any harm.

Darius shut the back door and headed for his bedroom. These past few days were a strain on his normally drama-free life. He kicked his slippers off and dropped on top of his king-size bed. The pillow-top mattress surrounded his body and hastened him toward sleep.

Jenna watched Teddy from under hooded eyelids. He was finer and more confident than she remembered.

"Thank you again for the black bottoms. I want you to share them with me. Did you want a glass of milk or something?"

"No thanks. You go ahead and eat them. I brought them for you to enjoy."

"Well, I'll eat them later. I can't remember the last time I've seen you."

"I've spotted you a couple of times when you would come home for winter or spring breaks, but you were busy with other people."

"I would have made time for you. Why didn't you call me?

"I don't have your cell phone number," Teddy said. He looked at Jenna's warm, caring eyes, and became bolder. "But you've always had my house and cell phone numbers. Why didn't you call me?"

"I…er…" Jenna stammered.

"I just figured when I didn't hear from you, our friendship was short lived. It was cool, I guess. Gave me time to concentrate on me and what I needed to do."

"What did you do after high school?"

"I was offered several football scholarships, but I turned them down. You know I wasn't into it that much. I just wanted to be around the cheerleaders."

"I remember the time I waved at you from the sidelines, and you went to wave back. That guy hit you so hard your helmet came off."

"I remember looking up from the stretcher, and you crying. I sat up and waved at you so you would know I was okay."

"The crowd went wild because they thought you were letting them know you were alright. That's when all the other cheerleaders started jockeying for your attention."

"It did go to my head for a minute. I will admit that. But you've got to know you were the only cheerleader I had my eye on."

Teddy reached for Jenna's hand and was touched when she placed her hand in his. He squeezed her hand affectionately and pulled her into a hug. When Jenna laid her head on his shoulder, both of them felt safe.

Jenna couldn't believe that she was lying on Teddy's shoulders. For years she denied her attraction to her friend. When she looked up at him, she knew she couldn't continue lying to herself.

"Jenna, I need to ask you something."

"Okay?" Jenna smiled and waited for the romantic words to slide out of Teddy's mouth.

“Where’s the bathroom?”

Jenna cracked up as she realized the fantasy did not play out. She looked at Teddy’s confused face and pointed down the hall.

“It’s down the hall on the left.”

Teddy reluctantly pulled himself out of the embrace and made his way down the hall. Jenna admired his tall, muscular figure and hoped they would have a chance to get to know one another again.

The doorbell interrupted her musing.

“I’ll get it,” Jenna called out as she walked toward the door. “Who is it?”

“It’s Detective Betancourt from the sheriff’s office.”

Jenna opened the door to a smartly dressed woman. Detective Betancourt flashed her official identification and did not wait to be invited into the home but pushed her way into the foyer.

“Come in,” Jenna said as she closed and locked the front door.

“Are you Jenna Judkins?”

“Yes, I am.”

“How are you feeling? Are you up to answering a few questions?”

“I’m good. Let me get my dad; I will be right back.”

“The report states you are an adult. Were the reports wrong? You don’t need his assistance to answer a few questions.”

“She may not need my assistance, but my daughter has the right to ask for whatever representation she would like, Detective. I’m Darius Judkins.” He extended his hand to Detective Betancourt who openly appraised his appearance. After an uncomfortable few seconds Darius pulled his hand out of her grip.

"Mr. Judkins you sound as if you were acting as her attorney. Are you an attorney?"

"I was an attorney. I no longer practice."

"That is strange. Everything I have heard about you leads me to believe you were common. I didn't know you had brains as well."

"Detective, has anyone ever told you that you can get more out of someone by being kind than that tough act you are pushing?" Darius glared at Detective Betancourt. His nostrils were flaring, his chest was heaving, and his pupils dilated.

Jenna looked at the two who appeared ready to face off. "Detective Betancourt you said you wanted to ask me a few questions?"

Teddy walked into the living room just as Detective Betancourt looked up. "Detective, what's going on?"

"Does everyone in this family have to date an officer of mine? What is with you women? Don't you know any non-police officers?"

Darius jumped from his seat. "That's it. I will not have you in my house insulting my daughter! If you wish to ask her questions, we can go to the station. You will not come in here with this garbage." He walked to the front door and threw it open.

Detective Betancourt stood to her feet and walked toward the front door. She turned back to face Jenna and smirked.

"Ms. Judkins, before I go, I just have one question. What is your relationship to Taurean Harris?"

Jenna's face turned bright red, her ears darkened, and her eyes widened.

"Taurean Harris is a friend of mine. I don't like that you are implying something different."

"Your expression indicates it may be something more than friendship. But I guess you don't want your boyfriend who is here to know that piece of information. Here's my card. Feel free to come answer my questions at the station where we will have more, um, privacy."

Detective Betancourt walked down the front steps toward her unmarked vehicle. She smiled as she let herself into the car and drove off.

"Pooka, what the hell is going on?" Darius demanded.

"Dad, I don't want to talk about this now."

"Mr. Judkins, Jenna, I better get going." Teddy looked around the room in order to avoid eye contact with Jenna.

"Teddy, don't leave. We need to talk."

"Jenna, I've got to go. We can talk later." Teddy shook Darius's hand and walked toward the front door. He opened the door, turned back to Jenna as if to say something but changed his mind.

Jenna ran toward Teddy, turned him around and hugged Teddy as if her life depended on it.

"Teddy, don't do this. I know it looks bad, but please give me a chance to explain."

"You know what Jenna. This is just like high school all over again. The last time Taurean's name came up, you said the same thing. Only difference was he was a big football stud then. This is getting old. I've got to get over you."

Teddy unhooked Jenna's arms, placed them at her side, and walked out the front door.

Jenna's eyes filled with tears. This is the second time in her life she wished Teddy would have listened to what she had to say rather than judge her. She laid her head against the door and remembered the last time.

Jenna and a few of her high school cheerleader friends were hanging out at the Seafood Festival in Havre de Grace. The sixteen-year-olds walked through the park and flirted with boys and older men. Feeling themselves or smelling themselves as her mother used to say, they made lewd comments to different men to test their womanly wiles.

"Hey baby, are you packing something in those jeans?" One of the girls called out to a group of young men standing by the carousel.

Another licked her lips, smacked them together, and smiled at the older man standing by the basketball game.

"Hey honey," Jenna yelled out to the broad shouldered guy eyeing her from in front of the vendor hawking "designer" sunglasses for $10.

"I know your mother taught you better. You shouldn't say stuff you don't mean," said a voice from behind.

Jenna turned toward the voice and almost fainted as she spotted Taurean Harris, Baltimore Ravens defensive player, standing behind her.

"Hi, I'm Taurean. What's your name little girl?"

"I'm Jenna, and these are my friends."

Jenna and her friends all talked to Taurean at once. He engaged the girls and acted as their escort the rest of the evening. He signed autographs for adoring fans. He watched the girls from a distance and ran interference when the overeager males attempted to take the game to the next level.

Taurean offered the four girls a ride home in order to make certain they each made it to their homes. He knew these girls were naive and had the potential to draw unwanted male attention.

Jenna was the last to get dropped off. She couldn't believe she had photos with her and Taurean. She couldn't wait until she told Teddy she met his hero.

Taurean pulled up in front of Jenna's house and got out to open her door. He escorted her to the front door and watched as Jenna opened the door.

"Thanks for bringing all of us home. You didn't have to do all of that, but I appreciate it. I will never forget it."

"I wanted to protect you like I wish someone would have protected my little sister. She was out hanging out just like you and your friends. She probably played the same little game with her girls, but one guy took her serious. He raped and killed her."

"Oh my, I'm so sorry. Thank you so much for protecting us. We were kind of silly." Jenna admitted as she threw her arms around Taurean's neck and he held her gently.

"Jenna, what the hell is going on?" Teddy demanded as he walked up on the porch. "I've been trying to reach you all night."

"Oh Teddy, look who I met tonight. Taurean Harris, Teddy Robertson."

"What's up little man?" Taurean said as he looked down at Teddy.

"Little man? Jenna, why did this old dude have his hands on you?"

"Teddy, I know it looks bad, but give me a chance to explain."

Jenna opened her eyes and turned toward her Dad who was still standing in the living room watching her.

"That was the second time Dad. Teddy's never going to forgive me for this. It's been ten years since I've seen him and we finally get a chance to get together, and now it's all messed up again."

"Pooka, it did seem like déjà vu all over again. I remember how broken up you were that night. You can fix this. You've just got to try a little harder to make him listen."

Jenna sniffled and wiped her tears on her Dad's Day-Glo t-shirt. Her Dad was always dapper when he hit the street, but around the house he dressed like he did when he was in college.

"Dad, where did you get such a bright orange shirt?"

"Pooka, don't you start. I had to wear stiff dark suits all day every day. Now that I don't have to work again, I wear what I feel like. Whether its Day-Glo shirts or cartoon pajama bottoms, I love it because it fits me."

"Dad, when are you going to tell Mom the reason you no longer work? You know she thinks you lost your job or got disbarred. Why don't you tell her you filed a lawsuit and are waiting for the disposition?"

"Darling, your mother would be trying to run my life and hers. I still love your mother, but she is a pain in the behind when it comes to employment. She would try to research the laws, review my case files, and question me a million times. Most times she's right, but I don't want that headache right now. So don't tell her. I'm not asking you to lie, just omit."

"You are a coward, Dad."

"You are right."

"I'm tired. It's been a long day. I'm going to lie down."

"Jenna, I forgot to tell you Roxie came by. It was strange. She said she was kidnapped the other day by one guy and another guy rescued her and dropped her here. She was in the kitchen waiting for you to wake up before Teddy knocked on the door. When you came out, she disappeared. Do you think she's on drugs or something?"

"Dad, Roxie is a lot of things, but she's no druggie. I'll try to call her phone and see if I can get a hold of her."

"Pooka, I know Roxie's your friend, but don't get caught up in her mess. She's from the streets and knows how to handle herself. You, on the other hand, tend to get yourself and others in trouble. Let the police handle this."

"Okay Dad. I'm going to bed. Love you."

"Love you, too. Don't forget to call your Mom. Tell her I said 'hi'." Darius closed the bedroom door. He walked through the house checking the locks and windows. He set the alarm system and turned on the outside motion sensors. He made his way to his gun safe and took out his forty-five. He cleaned the gun, loaded it, and strapped it on the side of the nightstand.

Jenna called her Mom but got her voicemail. "Hi Mom, it's me. I just wanted to let you know I'm okay. I'm tired and going to bed early. Dad says 'hi.' Later."

Jenna cut off the bedroom lights and hopped into the queen size bed. The sheets smelled of lilac, which always helped her sleep.

Teddy sat in his truck in front of Jenna's house.

"I cannot believe I fell for this again. Who does she think she is?"

"I can't believe you walked out of there. You still don't get it do you?" said a voice from the side of the truck.

Teddy drew his concealed weapon from his belt as he looked in his side mirror and pulled forward. He watched two very delicate hands rise in the air from the back of the truck.

"It's Roxie, silly. Put that stupid weapon down before one of us gets hurt," Roxie huffed as she came around the driver's side and jumped in the rear seat.

"Roxie, you could have been killed." Teddy's heart rate slowed as he holstered his weapon. "What are you talking about? How do you know what was going on at Jenna's? Were you there?"

Teddy put the truck in gear and started driving toward his home in Joppa.

"I scooted out the back door when Mr. Darius let you in the front. Jenna was asleep. I wasn't sure if it was really you or the people out to get me."

"Who is out to get you? What have you done now?"

"First things first. Why didn't you listen to Jenna? You know you love that girl, and she really likes you, too. You guys kept hitting and missing all through high school. Then you ducked her when she would come home from college. Don't you think it's time you find out the truth?"

"What do you know, Roxie?"

Roxie shook her head as a slow smile spread across her face. "It's not my story to tell. Teddy, give your girl a chance. Besides you've been waiting your whole life to be with her. You obviously love her."

"You are one to talk. You've never given any of us a chance to get close to you. I thought you and Jenna were like sisters, but you are never around."

"How do you know what I do? Are you keeping tabs on me or is it Jenna you are watching over? You're not stalking the girl are you?"

"No. I hear the talk from our other classmates. What is going on with you that has you hiding in my backseat? Any other time you would've jumped at the chance to ride shotgun?"

"Teddy, I can trust you right? I mean this is some serious stuff."

"You know you can trust me, the question is, can I trust you?"

"I was kidnapped two days ago from an alley in Bel Air. The person put something over my face, which knocked me out. I'm lying on some cot with my hands bound when it collapses. I yell out and some other person comes in and cuts me free. The person feeds me, tells me something about me, plays music for me, and then drives me to Jenna's house. On the way there, he tells me that I need to deliver three messages; one to you, one to Ms. Gertrude, and one to Taurean."

At the mention of Taurean's name, Teddy became enraged, shifted the car violently into drive and sped down the street. Roxie was thrown back against the.

"Teddy, slow down. What is your problem?"

"I'm sick of hearing that guy's name. What message did you have for me and that guy?"

"That's what I'm trying to tell you. I wouldn't know what the message was until I talked to the person. It would just come to me."

"Say what?" Teddy asked as he began to slow the car down and focus on Roxie's comments.

"When you started talking to yourself, I didn't know what or who you were talking about. But I prayed for the message and it came to me."

"So now you are telling me that Jesus kidnapped you, gave you a ride, and three messages? What drugs are you on Roxie?" Teddy shook his head as he tried to recall the symptoms of various drugs Roxie could have taken.

"I didn't say it was Jesus. What I'm telling you is that you are supposed to go back and talk to Jenna right now. Listen to me! It's very important you go back right now!" Roxie screamed as she pounded on the back of the driver's seat.

"I'm going to turn this car around. But you've got to get some help Roxie. We care about you and don't want to see you hurt."

Roxie leaned back, took a deep breath, and relaxed. She giggled to herself silently as she watched Teddy pull up in front of Jenna's house.

It was a little after nine o'clock in the evening and still light outside. Teddy walked up the front stairs and knocked on the door.

Roxie flashed the thumbs up to Teddy as she eased herself out of the truck. She crouched on the side of the truck as she watched Jenna's surprised face at Teddy's appearance. Teddy walked in the house just as Roxie crab-walked toward the car parked behind Teddy's truck.

Roxie hoped God would forgive the slight lie. She really only had a message for Taurean but thought if she mentioned Ms. Gertrude it would lend credibility to her statement.

Roxie wished her two best friends would get over whatever it was between them. It used to be the three of them. Jenna hadn't been the same since that night she met Taurean.

Roxie asked Jenna to explain what happened, but all she said was Taurean was a complete gentleman. Unsure of the facts but aware of the effect it had on the friendship between the two, she never questioned it.

Ten years was long enough. Roxie needed all the friends she could get. Roxie mused if she had to tell a small lie to get them together, well so be it.

Now she needed to find a way out to Havre de Grace. She spotted a taxi coming toward her and flagged it down. Roxie gave the driver the address the messenger had given her and relaxed against the back seat.

CHAPTER 9

Gertrude was in her office working late. As she closed her email, she heard her cell phone vibrating in her purse. She bent down toward her bottom drawer and heard voices outside her door.

"Where do you think they are hiding the documents?" said an unfamiliar male voice.

"I'm not sure. All I know is the person said the disk was in an envelope marked "application denied" on the top of the counter. They didn't tell us there was more than one counter."

Gertrude slowly made her way to the floor and sat down. She reached in her purse and retrieved Jax's business card. She quickly sent Jax a text message.

Gertrude thought this was the reason she had asked for an office with a front and rear entrance. If something was going on in the front of the office she could make her way out her rear door and go for help.

Unfortunately, they rewarded her with an office facing the street and no alternate escape route.

The voices sounded far away so Gertrude crawled along the floor toward her door. A shadow appeared in front of her door. Gertrude grabbed the amethyst rock she kept on her shelf.

The door eased open and a leg appeared in the crack. Gertrude swung the rock and connected with the kneecap of the would-be-robber.

"Awww," yelled Jax as he opened the door, and Gertrude stood up to take another swing at his head.

Jax ducked just in time, grabbed Gertrude and pushed her back in the door. He motioned her to hide behind her desk.

Two males were coming down the hall. The older of the two had something in his hand.

"Police! Freeze! Slowly put your hands in the air," Jax commanded as he drew his weapon.

Both men complied immediately. Jax walked over with his weapon trained on both men. He frisked them both.

"Call 9-1-1," he yelled to Gertrude.

"I called them after I sent you a text. I don't know what's taking them so long," Gertrude answered.

Just then two uniformed officers entered the office with their weapons drawn. "Hey Jax, what's going on?" called out the younger officer.

"Hey Johnson, we've got two suspicious characters that appeared to have broken in the HR office."

"Officer, I don't know what you are talking about. We didn't break in. We were called to pick up a packet and the door was open. We both work downstairs in Information Systems."

"Do you have identification?"

"It's in my inside pocket."

Jax reached to retrieve the identification badge of one Ernesto Santos, Information Systems Analyst.

"Sir, do you have identification as well?" Jax asked the second male who nodded affirmatively and gestured toward his pocket.

Jax reached in the man's pocket to find his identification, Justin Pickelford, Information Specialist.

"I'm not sure what is going on, but I'm about to find out," Jax said as he assisted both men to their feet. "Care to enlighten me?"

"I received a call earlier this afternoon from an anonymous source that there was information on a disk in HR about system integrity concerns. We've been noticing some blips on our server that shouldn't be there, but we can't locate the source."

"Once Justin told me about the call, we made the decision to come in here and get the packet. We didn't break in. The door to the suite was propped open," Ernesto said.

"Well I'm afraid we are going to have to take possession of that packet. It may have something to do with the kidnapping and beatings of your coworkers," Jax said as he held out his hand.

Reluctantly, Ernesto handed over the courier envelope. The two uniformed officers escorted the two men out the front door.

“Gertrude, it’s safe to come out honey.” Jax walked toward her office. He pulled a CD case out of the envelope.

“Let me see that CD Jax,” Gertrude said as she flashed all of her teeth at Jax.

“I can’t do that. It could have something to do with what’s going on and is part of the evidence. I need to take it into the station.”

“It could also have the answers to some of this week’s riddles, too! Let me see it!”

Jax resisted Gertrude’s attempt to get her way. He took her hand and pulled her toward the door. “We need to get out of here.”

Gertrude poked out her lips and pulled away from Jax. “I need to grab my purse,” she said as she lifted her purse out of her desk drawer. Gertrude shut down her computer and allowed Jax to walk her out of the office.

Gertrude looked down at the envelope in Jax’s hand. She knew that chicken scratch handwriting. Sonya had some explaining to do tomorrow. For now, Gertrude was content to enjoy Jax’s attention, but tomorrow she would begin her own investigation.

Jax and Gertrude were walking out the front door when Detective Betancourt pulled up.

“Just the people I was looking for earlier. I heard on the radio there was a break-in,” Detective Betancourt shouted through her window.

“As usual Detective you are loud and wrong. There wasn’t a break-in. Jax, I’m going to my car so you can deal with her.”

Jax walked besides Gertrude and opened the driver side. He quickly scanned the back seat and sat Gertrude.

"Be careful getting home. Give me a call the minute you get there."

"I will Jax. You be careful as well. I don't trust her."

"Can you two lovebirds continue this in a private place later? We've got work to do, Washington."

Gertrude rolled her eyes as she pulled her car from the curb.

Jax walked over to Detective Betancourt and handed her the packet. "The two men we found in the office received a call about the CD. They are employees of the agency who work in Information Systems."

The detective looked inside the envelope and closed it. "I'll get this over to the station and have someone give it a look."

"Well Detective, I better get going."

"Jax, can I ask you something?"

"What is it?"

"What do you see in that woman? Is it because she's tall or black or both? We have more in common than you and Ms. Judkins."

"Detective, I've tried to be professional and to separate my private life from my career. I would suggest you do the same. Have a good evening." Jax shook his head as he walked to his car. He didn't know why Betancourt didn't get it. He watched her drive away and put his own truck in drive.

Gertrude pulled her car around Hickory after she saw both vehicles pull away from the curb. She had doubled back around to the building after remembering Sonya hid things under her desk.

She parked in the garage across the street and made her way to the HR office. She swiped her identification card to gain access. She walked to Sonya's cubicle and squatted to look under her desk. She saw several bags and felt what appeared to be small travel size bottles, which she had overlooked earlier. She felt a hard case and pulled it to her. It was a CD.

"What are you doing here, Gertrude?"

Gertrude was so surprised by the voice, she attempted to stand, hit her head on the desk, and dropped the CD case.

"Jax, you scared the goobers out of me. What are you doing here? I saw you pull off."

"Well, I had a sneaking suspicion you would double back so I doubled back. Great minds think alike." He smiled at her and bent down to retrieve the CD.

"Whose desk is this?"

"It's Sonya's, the file clerk. She came to see me today and mentioned that she likes to hide things under her desk. She also told me someone put a wadded up, bloody cloth under there while she was at lunch. I called it in to Betancourt."

"Well let's take a look." He walked toward Gertrude's desk. "Can you turn your monitor so the glow isn't lighting up the window?"

Gertrude walked over to the monitor and turned it toward the door. She logged into the system and put the CD in the drive. There were three folders on the CD.

Gertrude clicked on the first folder marked "WTF." What she saw made her flesh crawl. The folder contained graphic images of her beaten coworkers Madeline and Worrell in compromising positions taken in the HR office.

"Gertrude, Stop looking at the photos," Jax leaned over and checked out the folder marked "Numbers." The screen filled up with scanned images of receipts from hotels, casinos, and restaurants all around Maryland, Delaware, and DC.

"Those receipts are for thousands of dollars and all using the same credit card. I'm not sure what we are looking for. There are more than a hundred different receipts dated within the last year."

"Let's look at the last folder. Click on it please."

The final folder was empty. Gertrude backed out of the folder to look at the folder views. She pointed her mouse toward the third folder and noted the time shown for the last modification. Gertrude gasped as she realized the last folder was modified at 8:30 p.m.

"The last folder was modified at 8:30. Someone was in this office while I was here and changed the folder. Everyone knows Sonya leaves at 4:30 every day. She's never a minute late. I've never known her to return to the office."

"So whatever was on the disk has been deleted. I hope Detective Betancourt's copy has all of the same information."

"Jax, I'm tired of all of this. I just want things back to the normal craziness. HR is rough, but we've never harmed each other."

Gertrude rolled her head around on her shoulders in an effort to relax. Jax walked over to her and began to massage her shoulders. It seemed each area he touched melted at his ministrations.

"That felt so good"

"You're tense. You've got to learn to relax, Gertrude. Don't let this job kill you."

"I know, but sometimes it's hard to separate work from home. It seems I spend so much time here."

"I think if you give me a chance, I can show you how to relax. How about this weekend? Do you want to go fishing out on my boat for a few hours?

Gertrude laughed as she stood up. "Jax, the last thing you want to do is take me on a boat to fish. I love the water but can't stand fishing. Now I do like crabbing. Or if you really like fishing, I can take my book and do some reading."

"Why don't you like fishing?"

"My parents used to take me fishing when I was a little girl. I was always afraid of worms like other little girls. But because I was so tall, they were hard on me. My mom used to yell at me because she said 'as big as you are, you shouldn't be scared of anything.' I don't know why my mom associated height with boldness. I guess only short people can get scared."

Jax held out his hand to Gertrude. She accepted it and the hug that followed. Jax surrounded Gertrude with his strong embrace and placed a gentle kiss on the side of her cheek. He could feel her soft sobs and pulled her in even closer.

"Look at me Gertrude. Were you scared tonight?"

"Yes, Jax, I was scared. I tried to be bold and I'm sorry for hitting you in your knee with my rock."

"I'm just glad you hit my good knee and I have quick reflexes. As hard as you were swinging you probably would have killed me if you connected with my skull."

Gertrude looked into Jax's big brown eyes and felt herself swoon. Her knees buckled, but Jax's strong arms kept her upright. He leaned so close to his face she could practically taste the minty mouthwash or candy he'd eaten earlier.

Gertrude pursed her lips just as Jax leaned in and kissed her. He wrapped her in his arms as he kissed her stronger.

"Wow! That was some kiss, Jax."

"I loved that kiss. I really didn't want to stop, but it's getting late, and I need to get you home."

"That's not necessary. I can get home by myself."

"Gertrude, if we are going to be exclusive there are some things you need to understand. I'm very protective of the people I care about, and I've come to care a great deal about you. Let me protect you. You need someone to care about what happens to you."

Gertrude's eyes misted over as Jax's words soothed her wounded soul. She recently prayed about the same issues and often wondered who would care if she lived or died. Jenna was grown and living her life. She had only one close girlfriend who lived out of state. Darius was too busy chasing women to care about his ex-wife.

Gertrude held out her hand to Jax and wove her fingers in his. "Thanks for offering to protect me. I think I will like that, but be patient with me. No one has ever offered to do that. I've always had to protect myself even in my relationships. I always sat watching the exits, parking in lit areas, keeping a knife under my bed. I've never been able to relax."

"Well stick with me baby, and I will protect you. We will spend time relaxing and getting to know each other."

Jax held the office door open and admired Gertrude's sexy frame as she walked out. He grabbed her hand and walked toward the front of the building. He led her toward her car, held out his hands for the keys, and unlocked her car door. He quickly scanned the inside before placing her in the driver's seat.

"I will follow you to your house."

"Okay, Jax."

Jax whistled as he made his way to his truck. *This day turned out much better than it began,* he thought as he started up his vehicle and drove behind Gertrude toward Belcamp.

Gertrude couldn't help glancing at her rearview mirror every few seconds to watch Jax in his truck. The man kept his word and was following closely behind her. Gertrude tried to remember the last time a man followed her home and realized it was after she and Darius divorced. He had started his law practice and needed some books he left in the attic. Once Darius fetched his things, he made like a ghost and scrammed.

Jax actually wanted to protect her, and it scared the crap out of her. Gertrude had always protected herself and everyone around her. She couldn't help it because it was always expected of her. Ms. Betty told her she had to protect her little brother because she was bigger than all of his friends.

Gertrude spent half her high school years fighting his battles against boys stronger and faster. She couldn't beat a man fighting fair so she learned to use weapons—bricks, sticks, and one time a baseball bat. She had battle scars that most girls will never understand. Her gorgeous legs have at least forty dark marks of different boys or men putting their hands on her.

Men who were supposed to love her only seemed to feel better when they had punished her for something or taught her was the man in the relationship. Love wasn't supposed to hurt. The God of all creation was a God of love. His love encouraged, supported, caressed, and uplifted.

Gertrude signaled to turn right onto her court with Jax following closely. She pulled up in front of her townhome and cut off her car. He pulled his truck into the space next to her.

To Gertrude's amazement, he walked up to her door and held it open. "Come on out, sexy. It's time someone showed you how to relax."

"Thanks, Jax."

Gertrude took the hand he offered and allowed herself to be helped to her feet. He reached in the back seat and grabbed her work bag and her purse. She opened the front door and turned off the alarm.

Jax stood outside on the front porch holding Gertrude's things.

"What are you doing?"

"I'm waiting to be invited inside, Gertrude. I would never presume you expected me to follow you inside."

"Please come inside, Jax."

Gertrude turned toward her foyer and hoped she was successful in wiping the surprised look off her face. He respected her space and her womanhood. All at once, Gertrude realized life with him was going to hold all kinds of wonderful and delightful surprises.

"You have a wonderful home. Where do you want me to put this?" He held up her bags in the air.

"You can just hang them from the banister. Do you want anything to drink?"

"What do you have to choose from?

"I have Coke products, iced tea, and two different kinds of juice."

"I'm a Barq's man myself. I'll take one of those, please."

Gertrude reached into the refrigerator and retrieved the can of soda for Jax and poured herself a glass of iced tea.

"Come on into the living room and make yourself comfortable," Gertrude said as she walked into the room.

Jax looked around the smartly decorated home. Gertrude's home was full of art, photos, and comfortable furniture.

"Is that a photograph of you and Wayne Newton?" Jax asked.

"Yes, I took that when I saw him in Las Vegas."

"Wow, Wayne Newton. I would never figure you to go for the lounge acts."

"Remember that old show *Laugh-In*? I saw Lola Falana on that show. She had on the sexy sequin gown, laid on the piano, and sang her heart out. The audience ate her up, and I wanted to be a lounge singer just like her. Needless to say, it hasn't happened yet, but I'm holding out hope."

Jax watched Gertrude's face light up as she reminisced and again felt he needed to do whatever he could to keep that smile on her face.

"You told me earlier this week you love all kinds of music. You never told me whether or not you played an instrument."

"I actually can play any instrument. It's a strange gift God gave me, but if I put it in my hand I can play it like I've studied my whole life," Jax admitted bashfully.

"That is awesome, Jax. Name some of the instruments you've played."

"I've played piano, drums, keyboards, saxophone, trumpet, cello, violin, harp, bassoon, French horn, flute, bagpipes, and oboe."

Gertrude sat down on the couch next to Jax and turned to face him. She folded her leg under her and watched Jax. She admired his talent and humbleness.

Jax gazed openly at Gertrude's face and drank in her beauty. He opened his mouth to tell her how gorgeous she looked but didn't want to waste words saying what his mouth could show much better. Jax placed his hands on either side of Gertrude's face and drew her to him.

Gertrude tilted her head. The joining of their mouths felt like heaven; it felt like coming home.

After what seemed like eternity, the pair reluctantly broke apart to take in some much needed oxygen. Gertrude smiled broadly at the man facing her.

"You are the best kisser. I really love those lips of yours," Gertrude hummed to Jax.

"I believe you put the kiss in kisser, darling. I enjoy you as well. Gertrude, I want to be your man and expect to be exclusive. I don't want to see another woman, and I don't expect you to date another man. If you can't commit to me, then let's not get it started."

Gertrude stared at Jax.

"Jax, don't you think it's a little soon to talk about being exclusive. You don't even know me that well."

"I don't have to know everything about you to know I want forever with you. I have the rest of my life to learn about you, but I want us to move toward a forever after kind of relationship. I'm not casual with dating. In fact it's been ten years since I've dated anyone. I'm no saint, I've had the one night stands and found them lacking. I've concentrated on enjoying my singleness by traveling and doing me the last seven or so years. I've been praying to God to help me find my wife and to recognize her when I find her. You are that woman. I've just got to convince you of the same."

Gertrude's shock was apparent by her open mouth and wide-eyed expression. She tried to process all Jax said and was having a hard time accepting it at face value.

"Not to worry. I will take it slow. I just want you to know I'm not playing games. So close your mouth, stand up, and walk me to the door."

"Hold up there, partner. You can't keep ordering me around like that. I'm quite capable of making my own decisions and will decide what I'm going to do."

Jax pulled Gertrude off the couch and kissed her passionately.

"Okay firecracker. You make your decisions. I just want you to know what my intentions are for you. Would you mind walking me to your front door?"

Gertrude couldn't help but smile at his boldness. She shook her head and walked toward her front door.

"I'm going to enjoy getting to know you, Jax. You are a breath of fresh air. I will agree to be exclusive only because I don't currently have any other gentlemen callers in rotation."

It was Jax's turn to be shocked, but he recovered quickly.

"Lock the door behind me, and set the alarm. I will call you when I get home."

"Yes sir. Be careful."

"Goodnight, Gertrude," Jax whispered as he walked out the door. He got into his truck, started it up, and waited for Gertrude to close the door.

Gertrude locked the door and set the alarm. She grabbed her bags and climbed the stairs toward her bedroom. The bedroom was her favorite room of the house. Gertrude removed her clothes and placed them in the hamper.

She walked into her bathroom suite and ran the bath water in her whirlpool tub. The six foot long tub sat high enough for Gertrude to climb up into and stretch her legs. She poured in her favorite bath salts, turned her radio to the jazz station, and rolled her hair while she waited for the tub to fill.

After rolling her hair, she walked into her closet and picked out a business suit to wear to work in the morning. She turned off the bath water and soaked in the tub while replaying the last few hours in her mind.

Something about the incident in the HR office kept needling her brain. Gertrude read a few scriptures and said her prayers. She moved from her chaise lounge to her king-sized bed. She had just settled on her pillows when her cell phone rang.

"Hey, Jax, are you home?"

"Yes. I enjoyed you tonight. Get some rest, and I will talk to you tomorrow."

"I had a great time, too. Good night."

Gertrude's eyes fluttered close as she surrendered to sleep.

Across town Jax was preparing for bed. He laid out his uniform for the next day's shift. He smiled to himself as he thought of the last few days spent with Gertrude. In spite of the chaos around them, they actually managed to end up in a relationship.

Jax said his prayers, thanking God for his protection and for introducing him to his future wife. He asked God to reveal the things he needed to say and do for Gertrude. Knowing his firecracker, he would need all the heavenly guidance he could get.

CHAPTER 10

Darius tossed and turned in his king-sized bed. He woke suddenly, looked around his room, and went into the master bathroom. He stopped in front of the vanity mirrors and ran a hand across his face.

"This has got to stop. I can't keep going on like this." He hung his head under the faucet and turned it on letting the water run over his head. He soaked his head for a few moments, turned the faucet off, and reached for one of the fluffy towels hanging nearby on the brass hook.

Darius occasionally had nightmares, but this one was horrific. Most of the nightmares stemmed from one incident in his life, which he tried to forget. Several counselors and hundreds of hours spent talking about it didn't make it go away. He tried acupuncture, hypnosis, and electric shock therapy, but nothing worked.

Gertrude had explained to Darius the only thing that would help was Jesus. If he sincerely prayed to God for forgiveness of his sins and promised to live right, he would be delivered from his nightmares. What Gertrude didn't understand was God was part of the nightmare.

Darius loved women, and they loved him. He met this woman, whose name he could no longer remember, when he was in college. He chased her for almost half of the semester when she agreed to go out with him if he went with her to church first. Darius remembered thinking 'how bad could it be?' so he agreed.

When he arrived at the church, the young woman failed to mention it was Baptism Sunday. The young woman handed him a white robe and told him to follow her. He changed into the robe and followed her and several others into the baptistery. The preacher asked if he was a candidate for baptism and rather than say no, he lied and said yes in order to impress the girl. The preacher gave instructions but Darius's attention was focused on the woman in front of him.

When his turn arrived, he repeated the phrases without paying attention. He was pushed under the water, but Darius forgot to close his mouth. He started to panic, but the arms were strong and held him under while saying words he couldn't hear. When they pulled Darius out of the water, he was unconscious. In his unconscious state, he thought he heard someone laughing hysterically at the sight of his near death. Someone began CPR, and he coughed up the water in his lungs.

Every so often, Darius would have a nightmare about the near drowning. But instead of laughter in his dream he would hear someone say, "This one is mine." Another voice said, "If he actually believed what he recited he would have belonged to me, but I don't know him."

Darius couldn't believe he couldn't shake that dream. He wanted to call Gertrude, but didn't want to intrude on her peaceful night. *Besides, it was time he stopped relying so much on her for spiritual guidance*, Darius thought.

Darius smiled as he thought of his ex-wife. He remembered the first time he met Gertrude Judkins.

She was walking on the college campus toward her Master's Degree class with her head held high and shoulders back. She didn't notice the effect she had on every man she walked by. Darius followed her to the campus bookstore where he watched her purchase a bottle of water and some breath mints. He couldn't remember the weak pick-up line he tried on her, but he will never forget her words.

"Baby, you must be this tall to buy a ticket to ride on this roller coaster," she said as she held out her hand above her head as she looked down at Darius.

From that moment forward, he made it his business to try to "catch" her in between classes. After weeks of trying to get her attention, he finally overheard someone call her name—Gertrude.

He walked up to her one day and said "Gertrude, I've been trying to reach you. I would like to find out if there are any exceptions this week for the roller coaster?"

Gertrude laughed and told him she would be willing to make a one-time exception. He took her out to dinner that same evening. They dated for six months before he proposed. She declined his proposal and told him she didn't want to get married again. She had been married once before, changed her name, and before the ink was dry, the man had moved on.

Darius convinced Gertrude to marry him by extolling his virtues, his manhood, and the clincher; he would take her name rather than have her take his. Gertrude couldn't believe he would become Darius Judkins rather than have her take his last name.

Darius completed his law degree and worked at a local law firm right after they were married. His first case became an overnight media sensation because of the involvement of his client with a local politician who was forced to take the stand. The politician ended up perjuring himself rather than admit the adulterous affair and resigned from office. Soon after the case closed, Darius found himself inundated with cases, clients, and a lot of unwanted female attention. He would often meet local politicians or other power brokers for dinner and drinks.

Gertrude attempted to support her husband, but their new daughter demanded the attention of both parents. Gertrude felt married in name only as Darius was drawn away from home night after night and when he arrived home often smelled of alcohol, cigarettes, and occasionally sex.

The final straw was the night Gertrude had to work late and sixteen-year-old Jenna arrived home to find Darius passed out drunk on the floor and a woman walking out of their bedroom with Gertrude's silk robe on.

After the divorce, Darius kept the name because his law license had the name, all his businesses were in that name, and besides, their only daughter shared the name.

Darius realized he was not going to be able to drift back to sleep. His overactive mind was reeling from memories, dreams, and the week's events. He pulled his laptop from his briefcase and logged onto the Internet.

There were e-mails from the law office business manager reminding him to provide a mailing address in order to receive his office items and last check.

Darius never returned to the office after agreeing to mediation in lieu of filing a multi-million dollar harassment lawsuit against his firm. For three years he had been sexually harassed by one of the partners. The firm's defense was Darius's penchant for women, his lack of morals, and his past indiscretions with alcohol. Basically the firm made it his fault. If he wasn't such a slut, she wouldn't have assaulted him, forced him to watch her undress in the office, and give him grunt work after he refused her advances.

Jenna called him a coward for not sharing the information with Gertrude. He had finally met a woman who scared the hell out of him and he didn't want anything to do with. She wouldn't take no for an answer because she heard of his reputation with women.

Gertrude would be all over that and would never let him live it down. She would probably say he deserved it for all that he did to her and the hundreds of women he chased. The sad part was Darius agreed it was his fault to a degree.

He thought he could charm her, use her, get a partnership, and walk away smelling like a rose. Unfortunately, the woman had other designs and was used to playing in the big boy leagues.

It started off with verbal recognition during staff meetings. One time, she called him up to the executive suite under the pretense of assigning him some research for a case. When he reported to her office, she sat too close to him on the couch in her office. She "accidentally" spilled her water in his lap and attempted to wash it off.

During dinner meetings with clients, she would have him seated next to her and rub her legs against him, innocently of course. Darius knew he was being chased and was fascinated by her mind, her attention, and her luscious body. But something wouldn't let him give in. He would find creative ways to turn her down or to make certain a witness was in attendance.

Three years Darius had put up with it because he knew no one would take his word over hers. The final straw was the night they returned to the office after winning a case. Darius assisted on the defense team and was carrying her bags into her office. She went into the private restroom and upon return was wearing a negligee, stockings, and heels.

Darius dropped her bags and walked toward the door. She beat him to it, locked it, and reached for his zipper. He grabbed her hand and told her to stop. She snatched his belt, pulled his pants open, and stuck her hand inside. She groped him for a few seconds while he dialed 9-1-1. He started to talk to the police. She ran inside the restroom and refused to come out.

He let himself out of her office and waited outside for them to respond. While he waited, he took photos of his clothes and his reddened private parts. The responding officers were suspicious but maintained their professionalism as he relayed the events. He requested medical attention and was sent to the hospital.

It took a year and a half of fighting it out in court, having his reputation dragged through the mud, and feeling emasculated the whole time. He was surprised by the number of men who told him "I wish it was me, I would have given her what she wanted and got mine!"

Darius couldn't believe he was a sexual assault victim. He realized he would never be the same, but he learned a lot in the process. He understood what women had gone through in similar circumstances. He also discovered that he didn't care for lawyers as much. He used to take pride in being an attorney, but after his experience, he wanted to do something else with his life. He would soon have the means and the time to figure out what that would be.

The morning was dawning as Darius looked out his back window. He had a meeting in a few hours with a financial planner. After the divorce, Darius had very few debts. He paid cash for his modest home and the three-year-old car he drove. He intended to set up a trust fund for Jenna, pay off all her debts, and give Gertrude a large sum of money. He owed her and wanted to settle the debt he felt he owed for leaving her when she needed him most.

Darius walked into his closet and picked out a pair of khakis, a polo shirt, and some sandals. He had donated all of his suits to a recovery house in order to give some men an opportunity to dress for success. The way he figured it, if the lawyer thought he was broke, he wouldn't charge him exorbitant fees.

He quickly showered and dressed. Darius wanted to make breakfast for Jenna before she had to leave for work. He walked into the kitchen and opened the refrigerator. He pulled out the eggs, ham, cheese, tomatoes, black olives, and mushrooms. He diced the ingredients, blended the eggs, and put together the makings of an omelet. He grabbed the potato bread and butter out of the pantry.

While he waited for the pan to heat up, he made some coffee, and pulled out the orange juice and milk from the refrigerator. He poured the omelet and flipped it skillfully.

Darius chuckled as he thought of Gertrude's breakfast disasters. *Bless her heart, she couldn't cook worth a darn but always wanted to make someone something to eat. Maybe I should give her some cooking lessons*, Darius thought.

Jenna woke to the breakfast smells emanating from the kitchen. She didn't stop to brush her teeth.

"Good Morning, Pooka. Did you brush your teeth?"

"Nooo…," Jenna whined while half asleep.

"Go back down the hall, and brush your teeth. You will mess up my breakfast omelet with that mushy mouth. Go on."

Jenna got up from the kitchen island and dragged down the hall toward the guest bathroom.

Darius shook his head at his daughter. Twenty-six years and she was still going through the same thing.

Darius went to the front door to retrieve the morning paper but was greeted by members of the press on his front lawn.

"Mr. Judkins, what can you tell us about your daughter's involvement with the disappearance of Helena Perkins?"

"Sir, how well do you know Taurean Harris?"

"Is it true your daughter is involved in a love triangle?"

Darius grabbed his paper, turned his back, and walked back into his house.

"Pooka, we've got to talk."

Jenna walked out of the bathroom with her toothbrush stuck in her mouth.

"Whashup, Dad?" Jenna said with a mouthful of toothpaste.

"Jenna, finish brushing your teeth, and come to the kitchen when you're done." Darius hurried into the kitchen and turned on the flat screen TV near the table.

The local television stations were all running variations of the same theme. "Former NFL star Taurean Harris' fiancée Helena Perkins was kidnapped. Jenna Judkins, former flame of Taurean Harris, was assaulted the same night."

Darius watched in amazement as the television reporters kept telling the same lies over and over again. The stations put up photos of the three of them all over the television.

Jenna bounced into the kitchen moments later with all of her teeth showing.

"Dad, Teddy and I straightened everything out and I think we are going to be fine. In fact, better than fine, because he asked me out. We are going to…" Jenna's statement was cut short as she looked at the TV screen and saw her and Taurean's face plastered on the screen.

"What is going on? I don't know anything about his fiancée's kidnapping. Daddy, why is this happening to me?"

Darius hugged Jenna.

"Honey, don't worry. We will get to the bottom of this madness. I just went to the porch and there are reporters camped all around the house. I better call your Mom and tell her you are okay."

Darius picked up the cordless phone just as it rang.

"Darius, have you seen the news? How's our baby?"

"Gert, I was just getting ready to call you. What in tar nation is going on?"

"I haven't a clue. I've got reporters parked out front. Jax is on his way to get me to drive me into work. I'm not sure if Jenna should go to work today."

"I agree. So you and Jax are an item? Good for you. I mean it. I hope he will make you happy."

"Not that it's any of your business, but we are getting to know each other. He's a very nice man who seems to be into me. I'm going to enjoy it."

"I will keep our daughter close, so don't worry about her."

"Thanks, Darius. I will give you a call later on today."

Jenna's cell phone buzzed. She looked down and answered when she saw Teddy's name on the screen.

"Teddy, can you believe this craziness. I'm not sure what's going on, but this is insane."

"I'm at the back door. I had to cut across three backyards to get here. Open up."

She ran to the back door.

"Thanks for coming, Teddy. Is it still crazy outside?"

"If you mean twelve trucks, a dozen reporters, and tens of nosy neighbors, then yes it is still crazy out there."

Teddy hugged her tightly. He whispered something in her ear, which caused her to smile brightly.

"Jenna, are you going into work?" Darius said.

"I just received two text messages telling me to stay home. It seems the reporters have staked out my jobs too."

"It seems you are no longer safe here either, Pooka. They have your Mom's house surrounded as well."

"Mr. Darius, I'm off of work today. I can take Jenna to my house in Joppa. I will keep an eye on her."

"Yeah, but who will keep an eye on you two?"

"Dad!"

"Mr. Darius, my mom lives with me because she is bedridden. She will be there to keep us chaste."

"Well I trust you since you've always looked out for Jenna. Keep my Pooka safe. Give me your cell phone number so I can get a hold of you."

Teddy gave Darius the number as Jenna walked into her bedroom. She grabbed a book bag, stuffed some clothes, her mp3 player, and phone charger into the bag.

Jenna kissed her Dad and walked out the back door with Teddy.

Darius put away the leftover food, cleaned the dishes, and went back into his closet. If he was going to make his national appearance on television, he wanted to dress the part.

He reached into the back of the closet and pulled out his emergency Giorgio Armani suit. He opened his watch drawer and searched for his favorite Clerc watch. He pulled on his square aviator sunglasses and slapped on some cologne to complete the look.

When he hit the porch, all chatter ceased. He made his way toward his garage. He looked around at the female reporters and smiled to himself.

"Gert told me to use my powers of persuasion for good, not evil. I got this."

CHAPTER 11

Roxie looked around the 3,000 square foot home and was unimpressed. She thought Taurean Harris's home would take her breath away, but instead it made her scratch her head. The man was reportedly worth millions of dollars but didn't have any furniture in his home.

She walked into the kitchen to scrounge up a meal but only found a few cans of Vienna sausages and some saltine crackers. There wasn't any kind of bottled water, but the refrigerator held a few cans of no-name lemon lime soda.

"Hey, Taurean, where is all of your food? Are you awake?"

Roxie walked out of the kitchen into the living room and shook Taurean awake.

"What's up man? Where is all your food? Did you give it to the homeless or something? Did you have a party?"

Taurean glared at Roxie from the couch. His head hurt, his teeth felt broken, and he couldn't remember who this pistol was with all the mouth.

"Don't look at me like you don't remember me. I found you busted up in front of your house and brought you inside last night."

"Thanks, I guess."

"What the hell is going on? You don't have any furniture, no food, your woman is missing, and you've been beat like an oriental rug."

"What do you care? You just happened to come over here and find me this way. You were probably looking to take whatever was left any way. Doggone scavengers— all of you!"

"I don't know who you are referring to, but I told you last night I was sent over here with a message for you. The guy told me you would need to see him to get the money for your fiancée."

Taurean broke out in gut wrenching sobs. Roxie walked over to him and slapped him hard enough to get his attention.

"I'm sorry, but I've listened to enough of your whining. I need you to focus so I can do what I need to do."

"You are one crazy woman. How do you know I wouldn't knock the stuffing out of you?"

"You are doing way too much crying to be some hard knock kind of dude. Besides, if you were going to do anything you would have done it before now."

Taurean sat up on the couch and looked at Roxie.

"Why do you look so familiar?"

"You know my girl Jenna Judkins."

"Who?"

"Jenna Judkins—lives over in Belcamp, you rescued her and her girls at the festival in Havre de Grace about ten years ago."

"I rescued a lot of girls that summer. It was the anniversary of my sister's death, and I was obsessed with making sure the girls made it home alive."

"Well I'd love to sit here and reminisce, but we've got to get going. The messenger will be here in a few minutes, so get up."

"What messenger? I'm not expecting a package."

"It's not that kind of messenger. Come on. Do you have your keys?" Roxie looked around at the near vacant house and shook her head.

Roxie pulled back a curtain to look for the messenger's car and noticed a lot of vehicle traffic out front. She focused her attention on the closest vehicle, which had the call letters for the local news channel.

"Oh shoot! There are cameras and reporters everywhere. We've got to go!"

Roxie pushed Taurean toward the back door as a shadow appeared in the doorway.

"Roxie, open up," the messenger commanded.

Roxie opened the door to her nearly seven foot tall hooded companion. His dark sunglasses hid his expression as he spoke to Taurean.

"I'm sorry for all of your trouble, but it will soon end."

Taurean looked up at the figure but couldn't determine if it was a man or woman. He didn't care either way. He felt compelled to go where the person wanted him to go.

The threesome left out the back door and walked straight into the backyard of a neighbor's house. The normally frantic dog that lived there observed quietly as the three stole around the front of the house and entered a waiting vehicle.

The dark colored vehicle motored through the estates at a leisurely pace to avoid attracting attention. The occupants of the vehicle appeared lost in their thoughts.

Roxie looked at Taurean and wondered how he lost everything. From what she remembered reading in the papers, he should be sitting pretty.

"Taurean, why are you living like you are homeless? What happened to you?"

"Why would you think you can ask me that question? I don't even know you. I appreciate you finding me and helping me in my house, but I don't owe you any explanation."

Taurean turned his head toward the window and looked out at the countryside and wished he could start his life over.

"You can't go backwards only forward. Wishing you could start over would only mean you have to go through the same things again until you learned the lesson," said the one Roxie called "the messenger."

"How did you know what I was thinking?"

"It was written all over your face. You are not a hard one to read," said the anonymous figure.

"Who are you, and where are you taking me?"

"Who I am is of no consequence. I'm taking you to those who wish to help you in your time of need."

"Oh hell no! I don't need some kind of intervention. Let me out of this car," Taurean yelled as he attempted to get out of the car.

"This isn't an intervention, and you cannot get out of a moving vehicle. Did you ever stop to think this isn't about you? Have you stopped feeling sorry long enough to realize your fiancée is somewhere out there scared to death and is going to die?"

Roxie leaned over and grabbed a few tissues out of the box on the floor of the car. She handed a few to Taurean as he began to cry.

"I can't believe Helena may die. I don't even know if she's ready to die."

"What do you mean ready? Who the heck is ready to die?" asked Roxie as she turned to the back seat to face Taurean. "That's about the most ridiculous thing I've heard."

Taurean turned to Roxie and shook his head. "Roxie, are you ready to die? Do you know where you will end up if you were to die right now?"

Roxie cut off the smart remark she prepared in response to the first question.

"I'm not sure. I mean I believe in heaven and hell. But I've got plenty of time before I have to think about that." Roxie looked at her traveling companions' serious faces and wasn't too sure if she was correct.

The car slowed as it turned into an industrial park. The driver pulled to a stop in front of a gate, which opened moments later. The car drove around the rear of the building into an area not visible from the street.

The three walked into the rear door and entered what appeared to be an office space. They were met by a gentleman wearing an overcoat and a fedora. He escorted them down a long hallway toward a set of double doors.

The group entered the doors and found themselves in a cavernous hangar. Roxie's "messenger" took off his hooded coat and revealed himself to the group. Roxie and Taurean both shook their heads. The man Roxie called the messenger was none other than Guy Blackman, a former NBA player, lawyer, and multimillionaire. Guy had disappeared from the public eye about five years ago. He was rumored to be in Cuba, South America, even Hong Kong.

"Guy Blackman," Taurean said. He held out his hand to shake hands with the legendary player.

"Oh snaps. I'm Roxie Vega."

Guy shook both hands and escorted them over to the couch.

"I know you two have lots of questions, but let me give you some information first. I want to apologize for the disguise, but I need to keep my whereabouts a secret. I know you two are wondering what happened to me.

"About five years ago, I was diagnosed with voice box cancer. I searched all over for a cure but ended up having my voice box removed. As you can hear, I still talk, but my voice sounds nothing like it did when I was an NBA announcer.

"I dropped out of sight in order to maintain my privacy and to handle my business interests. Thanks to the

Internet and cell phones, I can take care of my business anywhere in the world.

"Anyway to make a long story short, I arrived stateside earlier this year. When I arrived in Maryland, I looked up my old foster care mother Mrs. Cumbersome. I'm her estate attorney, and I usually stop in to see her every six months, but I hadn't been to see her in about two years. Unfortunately, she was in the final stages of pancreatic cancer. She made me promise to find all of her foster children and let them know she loved all of you."

Taurean and Roxie looked at each other and gasped at the same time.

"That's where I knew you from!" Taurean yelled as he hugged Roxie. "You were the little pistol who wouldn't let me sleep the first week you came. What were you—ten or eleven?"

"I was almost thirteen, mad at the world, and didn't trust anybody."

They both looked up at Guy at the same time when they realized Mrs. Cumbersome had died.

Guy saw the astonished look on their faces, walked over to them and enveloped them in his arms. "Mrs. Cumbersome died four months ago. She left all fifty of her foster children parts of her estate."

Roxie looked up at Guy and said, "Mrs. Cumbersome was the nicest old lady I knew. She was tough on us, but we knew she loved us. She was the first person I knew that thought kids weren't a nuisance."

Taurean wiped his eyes on his sleeves. "Mrs. Cumbersome saved up some money in order to buy me my first pair of cleats. She said she knew football would take me far, but Jesus would handle the rest."

Roxie began to cry as she recalled all of the wonderful ways Mrs. Cumbersome had treated her. One memory warmed her heart most of all.

"Mrs. Cumbersome once told me someone had forwarded my mom's things to me. She handed me a box full of scarves, old letters, and a worn bible. When I opened the bible, there was a letter from my mom. She wanted me to know she was sorry about what she had done, and she loved me. I knew my mom didn't write that letter, but the fact that Mrs. Cumbersome took the time to do something like that touched me more than she realized."

Guy signaled one of his assistants, who brought out a tray of food, drinks, and tableware. He watched as the two fixed plates of food and grabbed drinks.

"Mrs. Cumbersome was a wonderful woman and a smart investor. She never spent any of the money the foster care system gave her in the twenty-five years of offering care. She used her own savings and the insurance money left from her deceased husband to care for all of us. She invested her checks in stocks and later mutual funds."

Guy continued talking while taking in their obvious astonishment over his last statement.

"Mrs. Cumbersome's estate was valued over five million dollars after taxes. Each of you was due a check of one hundred thousand dollars," Guy reached into his pocket and handed Taurean and Roxie a check.

"I can't believe Ms. Cumbersome is dead. I know it will help me get Helena back but I feel awful." Taurean folded the check and stuck it in his pocket.

"You can have my money Taurean. It's what Ms. Cumbersome would have wanted."

"Did you two even look at the checks?" Guy asked.

Roxie looked at the check she held in her hand. The sum was for two million dollars. She screamed and threw her arms around Guy's neck.

Taurean looked at his check and his shoulders relaxed for the first time in days. As he breathed a sigh of relief, Guy thumped him on the back.

"Mrs. Cumbersome's will stipulated the checks only be given to the children who had tried to make something of themselves. Unfortunately, half were deceased, ten were in jail, and ten did nothing with their lives and were involved in illegal activities.

"Two declined to be contacted, so it only left the three of us. As her estate planner, I had to recuse myself. I gave one million to her church and other charities. The rest is split evenly between you two.

"Taurean, I've contacted a few friends of mine to assist you in the kidnapping. We are still trying to figure out what is going on and whether or not it's connected to you. From everything we've learned, I don't think it has anything to do with you."

Roxie slapped her head. "In all that was going on, I forgot to tell you about what happened to my friend Jenna."

"Roxie, we saw the news reports this morning and believe all of this is connected."

"What news reports?" Roxie asked.

"The reports say Taurean, Jenna Judkins, and Taurean's fiancée are in a love triangle, and the kidnapping is a result of the triangle. There were also reports Ms. Judkins was assaulted the other day and two of Helena's coworkers were assaulted the same day she was kidnapped.

"Do you think it has anything to do with the person that snatched me in the alley?"

"I'm not sure, but everything seems to center around that Human Resources office. My folks are checking on it. I'm waiting for a good friend of mine to show up and assist."

The three were deep in conversation when a gust of wind blew past them.

"Guy, why is it every time we meet it's got to be some spy type of stuff. Don't you have meetings at hotels like regular folk?" Jax walked up and shook hands with Guy.

"What are you doing here, Roxie?" Gertrude called out as she spotted Roxie standing near a tall gentleman who looked vaguely familiar.

"Oh God," Roxie said as she attempted to hide behind Guy.

"Gertrude, do you know this young lady?" Jax asked as he reached for Gertrude's hand.

"I sure do. This is my daughter's best friend who has been missing for the last week. What's going on, Roxie?"

"Jax, introduce me to your friend so we can all sit down and get down to business." Guy said.

"Guy Blackman, this is Gertrude Judkins. I don't know the other two." Jax said.

"Jax, this is Taurean Harris, Helena Perkins' fiancé. This is Roxie Vega, Jenna's friend," Gertrude said while giving Roxie the evil eye.

"What a small world. Why don't you two grab something to eat or drink, and let's settle down to business," Guy said. He extended his hand toward the fully stocked tray of goodies.

"Gertrude, do you still have the CD we found last night?"

Gertrude reached into her purse and handed Jax the CD. He opened his laptop, booted it up, and inserted the CD. Gertrude walked over to the tray, grabbed a Barq's and handed it to Jax.

"Did you want something to eat?" Gertrude asked as she fixed her a plate of finger foods.

"A Barq's is fine. Thanks."

Roxie stared at Gertrude as she ate her snack.

"Is Jenna okay? I tried to see to her last night, but Teddy showed up."

"Jenna is fine. You better hope this has nothing to do with you."

"Ms. Gertrude, I know you don't believe me, but I'm Jenna's friend. I would never do anything to hurt her. I've always been a good friend to Jenna. I was kidnapped myself, and I don't even know why. I was kidnapped by some random dude, and Mr. Guy rescued me and asked me to go talk to Taurean. I cannot believe all that's happened the last few days."

Gertrude looked at Roxie, and for the first time in a long time, felt compassion for the young woman. Roxie's eyes filled with tears as she looked at Gertrude. Roxie was vulnerable and all alone—save her friendship with Jenna.

Gertrude felt convicted of the way she treated Roxie over the years. The young woman craved Gertrude's acceptance. She walked over to her and hugged Roxie. The young woman's soft sobs indicated Gertrude had done the right thing.

The warmth radiating from Gertrude poured all over Roxie and provided much needed comfort. All she ever wanted was for Ms. Gertrude to act like she cared.

"Roxie, I believe you are a good friend. Jenna is fine. The last time I spoke to Darius he had sent her over to Teddy's house to avoid the reporters. Are you okay? You've had it rough the last few days."

Jax and Guy poured over the receipts in an attempt to find a pattern. Whoever used the credit card had expensive taste. Taurean walked over and glanced at the screen. He quickly reached in his pocket and pulled out his wallet. He pulled out a piece of paper and compared it to the screen.

"Those receipts are from my stolen credit card!" Taurean shouted. "I reported the credit card stolen a few months ago. I hadn't heard anything from the police."

Jax turned to face Taurean. "Think hard—what date did you report it stolen?"

Taurean looked at the paper and read, "It was January 12, 2011."

"These receipts are dated well after January 12, 2011. Are you sure you reported this particular card?"

"I think so. Helena was with me when I reported them stolen. This card had the highest credit limit, so we went online to report it."

Jax exchanged curious glances with Guy. "Did you report all of them online or only this one?"

"What are you getting at, sir?" Taurean's posture became defensive.

"Taurean, do you know your login information for the online account? You can check the status of the account." Gertrude said as she led Roxie toward the couch.

Taurean shook his head and took a seat in the nearest chair. Roxie walked over and spoke softly to Taurean.

"Where's the restroom?" Taurean asked as he shook free of Roxie's gentle touch.

"Straight ahead, first door on your left," answered the nearest assistant.

Taurean walked with his shoulders slumped toward the restroom.

Jax turned toward Gertrude and said, "I think Helena may be the key to all of this. What do you think, Gertrude?"

"Jax, I thought I knew the folks in HR, but I've since learned I don't know these people at all. I thought Helena was the real deal. It's hard for me to believe she would do this to Taurean."

Guy scanned the receipts and made notes on a pad of paper. "I may have something. There are a few receipts for the new casino down in Ocean City and the one up in Cecil County."

Roxie came running into the room. "Where's Taurean? He's not in the restroom."

"Roxie, calm down. I expected this; Taurean will be fine. He's trying to wrap his head around this whole thing. The whole place is wired with audio and video. My men will follow him and won't let any harm come to him. Keep in mind he will need to return in order to get the ransom money. He can't do anything with the check for days." Guy said cooly.

"Jax, why don't you take the ladies back home while I deal with Taurean? Besides, you don't need to be any more involved than you are."

Roxie and Gertrude rose from the couch. Roxie walked over and hugged Guy. "Thanks for everything. I cannot tell you how much you've changed my life in such a short period of time."

Guy gently cupped Roxie's face and lifted her chin toward him. "Remember all of the things we talked about earlier. You are worthy of all life has to offer. Be honest in your dealings with people. Most of all, believe that God has wonderful things in store for you."

Guy held out his hand to Gertrude and cupped her hand in his much larger one. "Gertrude, take care of my boy Jax. He's a kind man who will love you until time stands still. He will protect you with all that is within him. Love him as if your life depends on it."

Gertrude shook Guy's hand and placed a gentle kiss on his cheek.

"I will take care of him. Thank you for your help."

"Jax, come here and let me talk to you a second," Guy said. He motioned with his head for Jax to come over. Jax turned to watch Gertrude accompany Roxie toward the truck.

"I know you want to catch up and watch over her, but you've got to calm down son. You will scare that woman off if you are too intense too soon. She is the one who will guard your heart and defend you against all enemies. She is your complement in every sense of the word. Go slow, and don't hold her too tight or she will fight against what is in her heart."

Jax and Guy hugged and walked toward the double doors. Jax and Guy prayed for one another and thanked God for keeping their friendship. Roxie called Guy the messenger, but she didn't know how close to the truth she was. Guy seemed to be an open channel for the messages of God. Jax learned years ago to trust and believe what Guy told him. His riches never changed the man, and he gave away more money than some governments earn in the course of a year.

As Jax followed the women out, he couldn't help but wonder what brought Guy back to the states. His quick strides brought him close to Gertrude just as she reached the passenger door. He opened up the truck door and assisted her inside. Gertrude's smile of thanks warmed his heart.

"Roxie, you are awful quiet. Are you okay?" Gertrude asked.

"I'm trying to get over the shock of becoming instantly rich."

Jax and Gertrude both turned to their backseat companion. Jax spoke first.

"What are you talking about?"

"Mr. Guy just gave Taurean and I checks for two million dollars," Roxied said quietly. "I can finally pay back Jenna all the money I borrowed. I can pay off my student loans. I can stop living in my car. It somehow just doesn't feel real." Roxie sniffled and wiped her nose on her sleeve.

"Roxie, you were living in your car?" Gertrude suddenly became tearful at the mention of Roxie's homeless state. "I had no clue things were that bad for you. Why didn't you come to me?"

"Ms. Gertrude, you and I both know you couldn't stand me. You wouldn't have believed me anyway. I mean, it's not your fault. I know I've lied a lot, but I wouldn't have lied to you about something like that."

Gertrude felt ashamed and could not believe she had treated some woman's child as badly as she treated Roxie.

"I'm so sorry for the way I've treated you. I'm even sorrier that you were living in your car and didn't think you could ask me for help. Please forgive me." Gertrude choked out the words and prayed for God to forgive her as well.

"It's okay, Ms. Gertrude. I know you were protecting Jenna. I always wished I had a mom who would go to bat for me like you did for her. I'm just glad you never stopped Jenna from being my friend."

Jax reached over and gently took Gertrude's hand. He started the truck and pulled away from the industrial park. Jax turned on his favorite light jazz station to lighten the heavy mood. The music enveloped the traveling companions in comfortable silence giving each of them a chance to deal with their thoughts.

Gertrude felt Jax's rough hand in hers and looked over at him as he drove. Jax appeared in control, calm, and never fazed by anything going on.

Gertrude was reeling from Roxie's pronouncements. If Gertrude were in the car alone she would have pulled over and started bawling. A motherless young woman—a good friend to her daughter for half of her lifetime—was homeless, and she knew nothing about it. Roxie was rough, but she was a good kid at heart.

"Roxie, if you don't mind me asking—how did you become a millionaire?"

"Mr. Guy says Mrs. Cumbersome left us money from her estate."

"Mrs. Cumbersome died? I wondered what happened to her after you graduated. She just disappeared."

"Mr. Guy says she had pancreatic cancer and probably was in a nursing home since she didn't have any family. I lost contact with her when I graduated college," Roxie sadly said.

"Well, she would be proud of you. You've accomplished quite a bit, considering all you've gone through. I'm proud of you, too."

"Thanks, Ms. Gertrude. You don't have to be nice to me now because I'm rich," Roxie joked.

"You found me out. You know I had my eye on a designer bag and some designer shoes."

"Ladies, I hate to interrupt, but we are here."

Roxie and Gertrude both looked out the window at the beautiful home in front of them.

Gertrude turned to Jax, "Is this your home?"

Jax smiled brightly at Gertrude, leaned over and pecked her gently. "It is for now."

Roxie softly whistled in the back seat. "I can find somewhere else to hang out if you guys want to be alone."

Jax opened Gertrude's door then Roxie's. "No need, young lady. We could use a chaperone."

They laughed as they made their way to Jax's front door. Jax unlocked the door, turned off the alarm system, and turned on the foyer lights.

Jax's home was a study of contrasts. The outside was quarry rock, tile, and concrete. The inside was warm, comfortable, and decorated in earth tones. The bamboo floors massaged the women's feet as they walked barefoot across the floor toward the huge, airy kitchen.

Roxie looked around the large living room with thick carpet set under large masculine pieces of leather furniture. Wildflowers were placed throughout the room providing tempting fragrances, which teased the senses.

Gertrude walked toward the French glass doors and was pleasantly surprised by the outdoor patio and pool area. The granite and concrete theme was continued in the backyard. There were several chaise lounges, fire pits, and tables strategically placed around the yard. The privacy fence surrounded the backyard.

Jax opened the doors and walked Gertrude out to the patio area. He turned to the left and led her toward a private area just off the master bedroom. To Gertrude's delight, there was a large Jacuzzi, outdoor shower, and a king sized bed set under a portico. The area was only visible from the master bedroom.

Unspoken promises were made and acknowledged. Jax held Gertrude in his arms, and she relaxed against him.

"You have a wonderful home, Jax. I'm impressed."

"Thank you, but I'm more impressed by the warm, wonderful woman I'm holding right now."

"Excuse me, Mr. Jax. Where is your bathroom?" yelled Roxie.

Jax and Gertrude both laughed at the perfect timing. "Make a left out of the kitchen, first door on your right." Jax turned Gertrude toward him, bent his face to her and kissed her thoroughly.

He broke free and gazed at Gertrude. "I wanted to give you that before she got back. Ms. Roxie appears to take her chaperone duties seriously."

Just then, Gertrude's cell phone jangles the silence.

"Hey sweetie, what's going on?"

"Hi Mom, I just wanted to let you know I'm over Teddy's house. Dad sent me over here when the reporters showed up to the house. His mom told me to tell you 'hi.'"

"Tell Mrs. Robertson I said 'hi.' I've got your girlfriend with me."

"You found Roxie? Let me talk to her."

"I'll have her call you back. I want to keep my line open in case your Dad calls with some information."

"Gertrude, have you seen my keys?" Jax asked.

"Jenna, I've got to go. Something tells me your friend has disappeared again. Smooches."

"Smooches."

Gertrude strode toward Jax as he looked around the kitchen. "Jax, you can stop looking. Roxie has your truck."

Roxie walked into the kitchen with Jax's keys and handed them over. "I was going to take your truck, but then I realized I needed to make better decisions. I figured you guys wanted to be alone but were too nice to take me and drop me off somewhere."

Gertrude gestured to Jax to leave them alone. "Roxie come here. I know I've been unkind to you. It's going to take some time to get past all of this. How about we agree to make better decisions and just be kind to one another? You need to stick with us because you don't know who's looking for you or why. Don't you believe Jax can protect us?

Roxie shrugged her shoulders and sat on the kitchen stool. "I guess I'm just used to looking out for myself. No one else would do it."

Gertrude nudged Roxie with her shoulder. "I am the same way. I was always fighting my own battles and couldn't trust anyone else to have my back. I guess you and I are a lot alike. But Jax is a good man, and I believe he will take care of us or die trying."

"I would give my life to protect both of you. Trust, and believe me." Jax affirmed.

"Ladies, make yourselves comfortable. There is plenty of food and drinks in the refrigerator. I've got some work to do in my office upstairs. Feel free to wander around, watch TV or swim in the pool. I may have bathing suits to fit you."

Gertrude scrunched her face "I do not share bathing suits with anyone."

Jax choked on the laughter as he realized his woman was likely to say anything. "Gertrude, I keep several different bathing suits in case I have male or female guests who wish to swim."

Roxie shook her head. "Ms. Gertrude, you are a trip. Mr. Jax, I didn't get much sleep. Is there somewhere I can take a nap?"

"Come with me. I have several guest rooms to choose from." Gertrude walked into the living room and picked an overstuffed loveseat to relax in. She looked around the room and felt at peace. The home had soft music piped throughout.

Jax stood in the hall observing Gertrude as she looked around the room. Gertrude looked up at Jax. She patted the loveseat and scooted over.

"Babe, this is a magnificent home. It is very comfortable and has an air of peace. I feel like I've stepped into a warm embrace. I just feel so relaxed. This is the perfect place for a police officer or anyone else to come home to after a stressful day."

"I know what you mean. As soon as I pull up in the driveway I start to relax, no matter what's happened earlier in the day. I built this space in order to make sense out of nonsense."

"My job isn't as demanding as yours, but this would be the perfect place to unwind and just enjoy the company of a wonderful man." Gertrude smiled.

"I didn't mean me." She blushed as she realized her words sounded presumptuous.

"Well, I built it for me and my future wife in the hopes that we would want to spend the majority of our free time here."

"What happened to her?"

"There wasn't a "her" when I built the house. I built it for the wife of my dreams."

CHAPTER 12

Taurean walked through the industrial park with no direction or purpose. His mind reeled at the thought of Helen's betrayal. He trusted her with his whole heart, and she used him.

"God, why is this happening to me? Why did you allow her to come in my life to steal my heart and my money? I would have given her anything."

"You really are a selfish little boy," Taurean heard from behind him. He turned toward the voice and spied Guy silently jogging behind him in a track suit and sneakers.

"I am not a boy! I'm a grown man with grown up problems," Taurean yelled.

Guy stopped jogging and placed a firm hand on Taurean's shoulder to keep him still. "You are acting like a spoiled little boy in need of a spanking. I can't believe you're still whining about losing your money when the woman you claim to love more than life itself is being held by folks who want to kill her."

Taurean held his head down as the tears flowed down his cheeks. The moans rose out of his throat in spite of his attempts to stop them.

"Taurean, what is really going on with you and Helena? Something isn't ringing true about this whole deal, and I cannot help you unless you tell me everything. We only have a few hours before the drop off, and I need to get my men up to speed. We have to know everything."

Taurean took a deep breath and sat down on the curb. Guy took a seat next to him as Taurean began to spill the tale.

"I met Helena a few years ago, and she was this wonderful young woman who thought the sun rose and set on me. I thought the same about her. She started attending the church I go to, getting involved in the women's ministry, but she never seemed really connected to God. I would get little glimpses of things, which would indicate her commitment wasn't at the same level as mine.

"I tried to introduce her to some of the other single sisters in the church, but she would say they were jealous or too deep for her to talk to about some things.

"Looking back, I should have known something was seriously wrong. One day her car broke down, and she called me for a ride. When I picked her up, I noticed she had some lottery number stubs and scratch off tickets. When I asked her about it, she would say she picked them up for someone from the job. I told her what the Bible said about lots and gambling, and she assured me she wasn't gambling.

"Then late last year, I was invited to the grand opening of the first casino in Maryland. Of course, I took Helena with me. As a local celebrity used in the media campaign, I received a few hundred dollars' worth of chips, which I passed along to my fiancée. During the course of the night, Helena won a little over fifteen hundred dollars, and I think she was hooked.

"Earlier this year, Helena asked me to open a joint bank account so she could access funds for wedding expenses. Initially, I put twenty-five thousand dollars in the account. A few days later, I put another fifteen grand in the account. I called the bank because I didn't receive the last bank statement, and I found out the account was overdrawn."

Guy whistled and said, "Oh man, I am so sorry to hear that."

"That's not even the worst of it. When I asked Helena about it, she made up some story about losing the ATM card and being scared to tell me about it. I went to the bank and reported it stolen. A few days later, the manager shows me a video of Helena withdrawing over $300 dollars worth of marked bills out of the ATM with the stolen card. Of course, I didn't press charges."

Taurean paced along the curb. He shoved his hands in his pockets and ran his hands across his shaved head in obvious frustration.

"I tried to get her some help and even took her to an addiction counselor. Helena didn't think she had a problem. I've prayed for her and talked to my pastor, but I've lost my woman. I don't recognize this creature."

"Do you think Helena owes someone a large sum of money?"

"I honestly don't know what to think at this point. The last time I talked to her, I could hear some Spanish dudes in the background yelling. When I asked her about it, she said she was sitting at the light down in Highlandtown. She was supposed to come into work the next day, but I thought she called in sick."

"Did you get any other phone calls from her?"

"There was a late night phone call, but she didn't say anything. I could hear her breathing."

"What day was that?"

"Today's Friday, so it was Monday night."

"That gives me something. What's your phone number?"

Taurean rattled off his cell phone number and took a seat on the curb. Guy stood up and moved away as he talked to the person on the telephone. After a few moments, he gestured to Taurean and they walked.

"Where are we going?"

"We're heading back to my site. I'm having the guys pull your phone records, your bank records, the ATM videos, and the blue light camera videos from the Highlandtown area of Baltimore City. We need to see just what was going on. From everything you've told me, I have a sneaking suspicion your fiancée was helped to empty your bank account."

"You don't think she stole from me on her own?"

"I think someone has their hooks in Helena, and she may have been kidnapped because she tried to protect you."

"I have been a selfish brat. I cannot believe I spent this whole time worried about my money rather than Helena."

"You were being selfish, but I believe you focused on the parts your heart could deal with. You refused to believe Helena would be that cunning or manipulative, so you focused on the money. You love her, and its okay to love someone who hurts you. It doesn't make your love any less real."

Guy and Taurean jogged through the uninhabited industrial park as the sun started its descent. Two men moved in syncopated rhythm. The only sounds were running shoes hitting the concrete. Taurean was able to relax as the air flowed around and over them.

He prayed silently for Helena's safekeeping, her safe return, and for mercy on the perpetrators of the crime. Taurean felt he would seriously hurt someone if anything happened to Helena. He loved her with every fiber in his being and prayed that God would restore her to the woman he fell in love with.

Guy approached the loading dock doors, which magically opened when they got closer. "My folks are hard at work on this case, but I also have security watching the property closely. Nothing comes in this industrial park without our knowing it. I own all the buildings in the park and lease out several. Some house my manufacturing plants and others are filled with my employees."

Taurean shook his head as he realized he knew next to nothing about his childhood NBA hero. There was so much more to Guy Blackman than his stunning career. The man was an attorney, an entrepreneur, a financier, and mentor to young men and women.

Taurean noticed the staff as they walked through the huge space. The staff ranged in age from young adults to seniors in their "twilight years." Taurean heard various languages and dialects spoken by the diverse workforce.

"In my worldwide travels, I make it a point to visit the areas off the beaten path. I've a special place in my heart for the "throwaways" of society. In every culture there are those who are set aside or tossed aside because they do not fit the norm. The orphans, the lame, the blind, the HIV infected people. I employ them all, including brilliant hackers, pickpockets, and others who asked for the chance to change," Guy said.

"Mrs. Cumbersome taught me the value of seeing the good in everyone. I found a brilliant scientist wasting away in a Mexican prison cell. He's working on a substance to eat away ocean debris without harming the water."

Guy's face brightened as he looked at a pair of teens hunched over a bank of monitors.

"Taurean, I would like for you to meet Brick and Mortar," Guy said, motioning to the pair engrossed in the monitor activity. "These two young men are twins from Cameroon who stowed away on my yacht during a stop in Cameroon when they were nine. They have photographic memories and IQ's in the stratosphere."

"They are comparing the videos from the bank, casinos, and street cameras to see if there are common elements. We are looking for videos with Helena to see if there are people near or with her in any of them. If the criminals are smart, they won't be right beside her, but will appear in panoramic views. If they are there, these two will spot them."

The employees updated Guy on their progress. Guy was friendly, giving a kind word, recognizing their efforts, and directing the work. You could see the respect each of the employees had for their boss.

"Did you get any rest?" Guy asked Taurean. "If you are tired or just want to chill somewhere, I can have one of my assistants take you to a private rest area. They have a queen size bed, fully stocked mini-refrigerator, TV, video games, laptop, showers, and personal items. We are a twenty-four hour mobile operation, and I provide the creature comforts of home."

Taurean yawned and nodded. Guy pushed a button on the telephone. "Ms. Green, would you head to my office. Mr. Harris would like a rest area visit. Please set his timer for eight at night. Thanks." Guy disconnected the call and turned to Taurean.

"Ms. Green will escort you to the rest area. Get some rest. Someone will escort you back to my office at eight-thirty." At the mention of her name, Ms. Green appeared. The tall, shapely woman was dressed in a black, pinstriped skirt suit with black, high-heeled shoes.

"Mr. Harris, a pleasure to meet you sir." The Spanish lilt surprised Taurean. The woman appeared to be African-American, but her accent indicated a Hispanic background.

"Nice to meet you Ms. Green," Taurean said as they walked toward the rest area.

There were open kitchen areas where cooks took orders. A coffee shop provided caffeine and delicious looking pastries.

"Did you care to stop and get a bite to eat?" Ms. Green asked as she slowed her pace.

"No thanks, I just want to get some rest."

"Well here you are, Mr. Harris." Ms. Green swiped her card, and the door clicked open.

Taurean pulled open the door to reveal a room decorated as if in a five star hotel. This rest area was more like a suite. The inviting room had soft lighting, a huge bed, desk, and flat screen TV.

Taurean turned to say goodbye to Ms. Green, but she had disappeared. He closed the door that self-locked. The motion sensor lights anticipated his movements and lit the rest of the room. He headed toward the bathroom and was pleasantly surprised by the shower. The shower had four showerheads and a bench. The room was built to accommodate a wheelchair.

He walked back into the main room and lay down on the bed. He wished he had his Bible because he needed his strength. He stood up and walked over to the desk, opened the side drawer, and was not surprised to find Bibles neatly stacked in rows in the cabinet. There were several different translations as well as French and Spanish versions.

Taurean selected the New King James Version and began to read Psalms 91. For some reason, whenever he was in trouble or going through any kind of drama, the verses calmed him down. God was still God no matter the enemy, the battle, or the overwhelming odds.

After reading a few more Psalms, he got on his knees and prayed. He prayed for forgiveness; he thanked God for all of his blessings, including the news that Helena may be innocent. He thanked God for bringing Guy into his life. He began to war against the spiritual wickedness involved in this drama and prayed for God to be victorious.

He put the Bible on the nightstand and removed his shoes. As he settled into the bed, his spirit calmed as the Holy Spirit ministered to him. He felt the love and peace of God descend and cover him. He slept peacefully for the first time in months.

While Taurean slept, Guy and his team were working hard to get to the bottom of this story. There were reports streaming in from his contacts, which indicated the players were from two different camps.

Brick and Mortar found several videos of Helena Perkins and two Hispanic men. In one video, the three appeared to argue around the corner from a bank. Later during the same day, video showed the men paying for high value items in a store using the pin number.

The teens also found video of Helena Perkins at the Perryville casino cashier. The panoramic view picked up the same Hispanic men accompanied by a tall white man. The pair zoomed in and noted the white man had a scar down the left side of his face.

Guy sent the videos over to his security team to check the Justice Department records for matches. If any of the three men had been involved in criminal activities, Guy was confident his folks would identify them.

Guy had a taste for a banana split. He walked out of his office and headed for the cafeteria. He stood in line behind several of his employees and placed his order when it was his turn. He only had a craving for the dessert every once in a while. The best one he ever tasted was created for him at Boxcar Willies, a little shack up in Perryville. It was a modest place, but he loved the food. One of his employees told him about another ice cream place, Broom's Blooms in Harford County, but he hadn't an opportunity to try their ice cream.

Guy collected his dessert and sat at a table in the common area. He was a frequent sight as he wasn't a standoffish kind of person. He enjoyed his life and enjoyed spending time with the people who worked for him. Guy counted his blessings as he ate his dessert. As always, the food was gone long before he finished counting.

"Sir, I hate to disturb you, but you need to see this." JJ, one of his security detail men, stood by waiting for a response.

"No problem, JJ. I will be right there."

"Yes, sir." JJ turned and walked toward the secured space.

"Hold the door," Guy called to him as he strode within two steps of JJ.

JJ wondered to himself how the old guy did it. Not only did he sneak up on him, but he had also covered the distance in half the time it took JJ to walk it.

"I have longer legs than you do," Guy remarked. When he entered the room, the chatter ceased.

"What did you guys find?"

"Well sir, it seems we have stumbled onto some serious stuff. Ms. Perkins appears to have been kidnapped as a result of some gambling debts owed by one of her coworkers."

Guy's eyebrows raised in obvious surprise. "This is getting stranger by the second. She was kidnapped over someone else's debts?"

Donna stood up and said, "Sir, from what I can gather, Ms. Perkins isn't a serious gambler. The night of the grand opening was the first and only time Ms. Perkins gambled at the casino on her own. According to her bank records, Ms. Perkins saved her earnings."

Guy turned to Donna and listened intently to his security analyst.

"We were able to identify one of the gentlemen in the video through the Justice Department Records." Donna looked down at her notes and continued speaking.

"Miguel Fernandez was captured on several of the casino cameras as well as appearing in the video at the bank. I pulled his files, and it appears Mr. Fernandez is a petty criminal with a penchant for losing big. His family has stopped financing his craving for the big payout. His bank accounts are overdrawn, his retirement accounts have been zeroed out, and his house is in foreclosure."

"The third gentleman's face is obscured, but his scar came through clear so the identification may take a little longer."

"Good job, everyone. Do me a favor; compare the unknown second Hispanic gentleman with the HR records. Also, run the rest of that agency's employees through the database. There is something else going on over there, and I believe it may be connected to other employees. I appreciate all of your efforts."

Guy rose from his seat and walked out of the secured space. He recalled Jax mentioning two men roaming around the office late at night. Guy pulled out his cell phone and dialed his friend's number.

"This is Jax, and considering the company I'm keeping, it better be good."

"You know there is such a thing as caller ID. If you looked down at the phone, you would know it is me," Guy said, chuckling.

"Hey, Guy. I would recognize that voice anywhere. What's up?"

"Remember the guys you caught in Gertrude's office. What were their names?"

"Gertrude's here, let me ask her. Babe, what were the names of those two clowns I caught prowling in your office?"

"Justin Pickelford and Ernesto Santos. Why?"

"Guy's calling for information. He's probably got something."

"Jax, tell Gertrude I said hi, and thanks for the info. We've got some serious leads. When are you due back at the station?"

"I work tomorrow. Do you have any leads on the Perkins case?"

"None I care to disclose to you at this time. I will be in touch."

"Well keep in mind Detective Betancourt is assigned to this case, and we both know you are not one of her favorite people."

"The detective's memory is short. She forgets that I saved her life. I know she wished it was you kicking in the door and shooting her kidnapper. At least she lived."

Jax laughed and disconnected the call. He turned back to Gertrude, wrapped her in his arms, and lowered his mouth.

Just as their lips touched, Roxie walked out to the patio and cleared her throat.

"Were you this annoying as a small child?" Jax asked.

Gertrude claimed Jax's mouth and took his breath away.

Jax broke free and placed his arm around Gertrude's waist. "Ladies, let's go back inside. Why don't you two get settled in the basement while I fix dinner? I have a vast movie collection you can peruse while I get everything set up. Do either of you have food allergies?"

"I'm allergic to black pepper. It gives me migraines. Did you need some help, Jax?" Gertrude asked.

"I'm allergic to bad food," Roxie piped in.

"No I don't need any help, now scat." Jax motioned the pair out of his kitchen.

Jax started his dinner preparations even as he wondered about Guy. His vast network of information was legal, but he couldn't help but wonder if he violated any piracy or privacy laws. Guy managed to keep Jax out of everything he did because of their longstanding friendship. He just hoped he wasn't ever forced to testify against him.

While Jax puttered around his kitchen preparing dinner for his guests, Gertrude and Roxie were walking around his basement stupefied.

"Ms. Gertrude, how many instruments does this guy have? He's got a piano, drums, keyboards, some kind of long, woodwind instrument, harp, and lots of other things I don't know."

"Jax told me he can play anything he touches." They left the music room and walked into the entertainment theater. There were Italian leather chairs arranged in elevated rows similar to a movie theater. The chairs faced a 60-inch flat screen TV mounted on the wall. They browsed the movies, which lined a wall on the right side of the room.

"Do you feel like comedy, drama, or sci-fi?" Roxie asked Gertrude.

"We've had enough drama, and I've had enough action. I need a good laugh."

Roxie picked out a comedy about two men traveling together while trying to get home for the holidays. "I've never seen this movie. Is it any good?"

Gertrude looked up from her movie case and walked over to Roxie. "This is a classic, full of laughs. I think this is what we need after the last few days. Oh yeah, before I forget, please call Jenna. She wanted to speak to you earlier, but I told her I would have you call her."

"I called her, but she didn't answer, so I left a message."

"I'm glad you are her friend Roxie. You were always a good friend, and I didn't see it before. All the other so-called friends of hers have fallen to the wayside, but you've been faithful."

"I've always considered Jenna my sister. If I had one, I would have looked out for her like I looked out for Jenna."

"Are we going to continue this love fest, or are we going to eat dinner?" Jax said as he walked into the room toward a door set into the left side of the living room. He pulled the door up to reveal steaming dishes of food.

"Is that a dumbwaiter?" I've never seen one in real life. I always thought they were neat." Gertrude gushed as she walked over to assist Jax.

"When I had the house built, I put it in. I remember always going up and down the stairs in my parents' home as a kid, thinking if we had one I wouldn't have to carry my snacks downstairs and the empty dishes back upstairs. So I installed one in my home. It's very convenient."

"Why didn't you get an electronic version?" Roxie asked.

"The builder asked me the very same thing. I told him in case the power went out, I still wanted to be able to get my food. He suggested a backup generator. We compromised, he put in the generator, and I have my pulley system."

"Jax, you are something else." Gertrude walked over to the middle seat and placed her food on the built in tray table. As she began to say grace, she quickly sobered.

"While we are getting ready to chill out and eat some great food, I can't help but wonder about Helena and Taurean. He will have to meet the kidnappers in a few hours. Will Helena live or die? What if they kill both of them and take the money?"

Jax sat next to Gertrude and took her in his arms. "Babe, Guy is all over this case. With his vast network of resources, manpower, and armament, he will make sure to return them safe and sound. I'm more worried about my guys getting caught in the middle and getting hurt. Knowing Guy, he's probably briefing Detective Betancourt and the Feds."

Guy hung up the phone with his local FBI contact. The agency could not afford to allow rogue players to interfere with an agency investigation. However, if the players were to assist in the efforts, the agency would appreciate it. Guy provided some information that the FBI hadn't yet discovered.

The next call wasn't going to go as well. Guy was dreading the call to Detective Betancourt. The woman was fixated on his buddy, Jax, who didn't care if the detective lived or died. Guy found the woman fascinating, gutsy, and a livewire. The only problem was she despised him. Guy laughed to himself as he dialed the familiar number.

"Detective Betancourt speaking."

"Detective, I hope all is well with you. This is Guy Blackman."

The detective yelled at Guy, cursed his heritage, education, and his birth. Guy listened enraptured by the sound of her voice.

"Bonjour, ma femme courageuse belle. I've missed you, too, my spunky woman," Guy said. "Let's not waste any more time. I'm calling to offer my assistance with the Perkins disappearance."

"I don't need or want your kind of help. I know you are used to the federal lapdogs turning tricks to be in your presence, but I'm not participating in the dog and pony show. My men are more than competent to handle this case."

"Well I look forward to seeing you later tonight. Wear something feminine and frilly for me. Adios mujer de mi corazon, goodbye, woman of my heart." Guy teased as he disconnected the call.

The hostile detective had no idea she was the woman of his heart. He met thousands of women in his travels and in business, but only one woman managed to worm her way into his heart.

Guy prayed he wouldn't have to risk his life for hers again. But he knew if it came down to it, he would take a bullet for the fiery redhead. *God help him,* Guy thought, *I'm a goner.*

Guy continued to make phone calls, coordinate manpower, and brief his personnel. As his small, mobile force moved resources into waiting armored vehicles, he prayed over them asking for God's protection and no loss of life.

A slight tapping sound caught Guy's attention. He spotted his security analyst standing at the door.

"Donna, come in."

"Sir, we've received identification of the third man. It's Gerasiim Ivanov."

Guy's eyebrows furrowed and he closed his eyes. After a few moments he spoke to Donna.

"When did he arrive stateside? I thought he was serving a life sentence in the Russian prison outside of St. Petersburg."

"According to our records, he was released in late 2007 after the reforms of the Russian Federal Prison system. He was allowed to enter the United States after his sponsorship by the Russian consulate. He is supposed to be a restaurateur on the eastern shore."

"Where exactly is his restaurant?" Guy asked.

"According to our records, it's located along Highway 50 just outside of Ocean City."

"Are you telling me an aging Russian Mob boss is running a restaurant within a few miles of one of our new casinos, and no one knows about it? Something is fishy."

Guy started to dial his FBI contact and changed his mind.

"Donna, are your people in place out in Havre de Grace?"

"Yes, sir. I have the skateboarders riding the promenade taking video of the visitors. We have two of our teens working in the ice cream stand and one selling bottles of water fifty feet from the lighthouse."

Guy had several teens and youthful looking security detail employees strategically placed around the city. He also called up a few markers from some unsavory folks he knew around town. He had the city on lock-down long before the FBI put their conspicuous group of people around.

"Do we have the frog men in the water?"

"Not yet—the water's been too choppy, but they are on the boats awaiting orders. We have the five mile circumference wired for sight and sound."

"Thanks, Donna. I've got a few phone calls to make before we get moving." Donna walked out of the office and nodded at the approaching Taurean.

Guy waved Taurean into the office as he finished the phone call.

"Taurean, we've discovered quite a bit of information. I believe it would be better for you to remain here with the skeleton crew."

"Guy, that's my future wife they are holding. Besides, they are expecting me to deliver the ransom."

"Taurean, it may get dangerous out there. I don't think I could forgive myself if something happened to you, son."

Taurean blinked rapidly. "Sir, no disrespect intended, but I'm going out there to get my woman. God told me to go, and I've got on my armor, and I'm ready."

"Well then sit down, and let me tell you what we know." Taurean took a seat as Guy explained the latest information.

"Are you telling me the Russian mob is holding Helena?"

"We don't know, but it is a strong possibility since it seems her coworkers are involved and were caught on camera with Gerasiim."

"I want to know how the heck Helena got caught up in this mess. I cannot believe this is happening to us."

"Taurean, I'm going to need you to stay focused and follow directions. Ms. Green is coming to escort you to change your clothes. You will be outfitted with a bulletproof shirt with electronic surveillance built in. We no longer "wire" anyone in this organization. One of our scientists has created electronic devices woven into the fabric of garments. The electronics do not have any metal parts and are not detectable if the person is frisked."

Ms. Green arrived on cue and walked Taurean toward the outfitters. Guy reached into his drawer and pulled out his weapon. The Ruger was a lightweight, compact pistol but was accurate and deadly.

Guy wasn't planning to be in the midst of action but better to be safe than sorry. He strapped one to his ankle and the other was placed in the holster on his belt, which resembled a cell phone case.

Guy walked over to his hidden wall safe and pulled out the duffle bag inside. The bag held the two million dollars in marked bills. The duffle was wired with cameras woven into the fabric to capture 360 degrees. The handles were coated with a lightweight polymer to capture fingerprints.

Guy zipped his track suit and walked out to the waiting crew. As always the group held hands and prayed for God's protection, guidance, and mercies for their enemies. The group disbanded and made their way to the waiting vehicles.

Taurean and Guy sat in the rear seat of the first dark colored SUV. The interior held monitors, which transmitted video from the cameras located along the outside of the trucks. The video feed captured the videos from the caravan's trucks.

Two motorcycles pulled up alongside the truck holding Taurean and Guy. The rider was wearing a tight, black, leather outfit, which hugged her curves. Ms. Green pulled off her helmet, said something to the other rider, and put her helmet on. The motorcyclists pulled off and raced out of the industrial park.

The caravan split up and made their way toward Havre de Grace along all incoming routes. Taurean's truck rumbled down Route 40. A few pulled onto I-95 North and headed toward the city. A couple made their way along Route 155 toward Havre de Grace.

Guy made and received several phone calls during the trip. When they neared Aberdeen, Guy hung up the phone and turned toward Taurean.

"Here's the plan. We are going to drop you off in the shopping center right off of Route 40. Ms. Green will meet you in the parking lot, and you will ride on her motorcycle into the park. She's going to drop you off in front of the ice cream stand at the entrance of the promenade."

"I thought I was going to meet them at the lighthouse?" Taurean asked.

"That's where they want you to meet, but there are too many exits. We will let the local police handle the lighthouse. When the kidnappers call your cell phone, tell them there were too many cops over there, and you are changing the location. We are going to have several of our conspicuous vehicles around the park closer to the lighthouse to confirm your story."

"Guy, I'm not sure I can deal with all this subterfuge."

"Taurean, I'm going to walk you through this thing. You said you were going to get her back, and you will. Trust and believe you will get her back safe and sound."

Guy and Taurean continued talking as they made their way toward the shopping center.

"I want to warn you in advance you will most likely not see Helena during the exchange."

"So I'm supposed to just hand off some money and not get my girl back?" Taurean asked in amazement.

"Just give them the money. Don't look back. Walk toward the ice cream shack, and sit down at the table in front of the window. If there are gunshots, duck under the table. The girl in the shack will return fire and protect you."

"How will I get out of there?"

"It depends on how this plays out. I'm expecting the pickup guy to make his way toward his escape. We do not intend to stop him from getting away. He's a decoy. Normally someone will approach you and let you know how to get the girl. We are watching everything. We've got air, land, and sea support, so try not to overreact. We need you nervous but not panicky. I'm trying not to give you too many details because we are counting on your responses to be natural."

Guy placed his hand on Taurean's shoulder as he prayed for him.

"Go with God, my brother. All will be well."

Taurean got out of the truck and walked over to Ms. Green's waiting motorcycle. He put on the extra helmet and placed the duffle bag over his shoulders. Ms. Green motored out of the parking lot and made her way toward the park in Havre de Grace.

Ms. Green pulled up in the parking lot near the boat docks. Taurean dismounted and handed the helmet back to Ms. Green. She pulled off and made her way to the rendezvous point.

Taurean looked around the tranquil surroundings and felt out of place. The waning daylight and the overhead lights made the whole scene seem surreal. He silently prayed as he made his way to the ice cream shack where dozens of families stood in line to order treats.

"Would you like a smoothie sample?" The young employee approached Taurean and made eye contact.

"Would you like a smoothie to take your mind off of your troubles, sir?"

Taurean realized the young woman was one of Guy's employees. She smiled broadly at him and offered a smoothie sample. "Keep the cup pointed toward the crowd but don't drink all of it," she said as she made her way back to the shack.

After an agonizing half an hour of sitting and people watching, Taurean's cell phone rang. He quickly pulled it out of his pocket.

"I see you didn't follow our directions, Mr. Harris," the male voice harshly said.

"There were too many cops up there. I figured you wanted to make the pickup away from prying eyes," Taurean answered as Guy instructed earlier.

"Well good for you for thinking about us. Your fiancée will be returned to you as soon as I have my money. Walk toward the promenade. I'm the guy in the white t-shirt."

Taurean stood up and began to walk toward the promenade. He took the duffle bag from around his shoulders. As he walked swinging the bag, a kid on a skateboard shot out in front of him, and he tripped. The man in the white t-shirt turned and suddenly walked away.

"Hey man, where are you going?" Taurean cried out.

"Don't worry about him. Worry about me," said the voice behind Taurean.

Taurean turned as the man behind him reached for the bag. The pickup guy was a nondescript white male of average height and weight with nothing remarkable about him.

"I'm your caller. The other guy was a decoy just in case you decided to be stupid and involve the police."

Taurean handed over the bag and turned to walk toward the table.

"Where are you going, Mr. Harris?"

"I'm going to wait over there for my woman. You said when I gave you the money, I would get her. I'll be over there," Taurean pointed at the empty picnic table.

"We will be in touch."

The man walked quickly toward the boat docks and slipped onboard a motorboat. The engine gunned as the boat pulled out of the docks toward the Susquehanna River.

Taurean walked over to the ice cream stand and ordered a soda. He paid for the soda and returned to his seat. As he waited, he prayed for patience, deliverance of Helena, and a return of his sanity.

Taurean watched as the shack workers cleaned up, emptied trash, and locked up for the night. Guy's employee headed over to the table.

"You can go on over to Ms. Green's motorcycle. You are done for now. Be cool and know we are praying." The young woman made her way to the rusted out Ford pickup truck and started the vehicle.

Taurean took one last look around the empty parking lot. His shoulders slumped as he realized Helena wasn't going to appear. He mounted the motorcycle and put on the helmet Ms. Green offered him.

No words were spoken as Ms. Green took a circuitous route back to the industrial park. There were several SUV's bearing different agency logos in the parking lot.

Taurean slowly made his way up the loading dock stairs. His mind reeled at the thought of never seeing Helena again. He would have given his life to bring her back alive.

Taurean was delirious and coming off an adrenaline high.

"Taurean," a voice so like Helena's penetrated the fog.

Taurean was hit by what felt like a football player. He looked down just as Helena wrapped her arms around him.

"Helena," Taurean cried as he held his fiancée in his arms. The two spoke in unison and alternated between crying and laughing.

Helena's successful return was miraculous. The skateboarder who bumped into Taurean was one of Guy's security men. It turned out when the skateboarder bent down on the side of a white van to tie his shoe and heard a muffled cry. He didn't follow his instincts and attempt to gain access to the van. Instead, he rendezvoused with one of the other employees and provided the description and license plate.

A few moments later, an elderly gentleman was spotted walking his dog near the van. The dog began to move quickly away from the vehicle, which indicated no explosives. If the dog had smelled explosives, it would have sat and waited for a reward. The man signaled the team, which created several diversions.

The team found a woman tied up in the van. They quickly removed her and placed her in a service truck that pulled up to replace the tire of the vehicle next to it.

Guy walked over to the couple and introduced himself to Helena.

"Ms. Perkins, I'm Guy Blackman. I'm glad you are well. I know you have been waiting to see your fiancé, but we need to debrief you as quickly as possible."

Guy turned to Taurean, who hugged Helena briefly and handed her over. Guy walked Helena toward a group of federal officers and left her in the capable hands of Ms. Green.

Taurean walked over to Guy and grabbed him in a bear hug. Tears rimmed his eyes as he attempted to share his appreciation and awe over all that occurred in an effort to bring Helena home.

The FBI and the local police began to question Helena about the circumstances surrounding her kidnapping. Helena looked around the room at each of the officers and began her story.

On Monday evening, she headed from her weekly acupuncture appointment. The doctor's office was located in Highlandtown near Eastern Avenue.

As she drove toward Interstate 895, she thought she saw Miguel Fernandez, a coworker from the agency, arguing with someone. She continued driving but noticed him running behind her vehicle trying to flag her down. She slowed and rolled her window down.

"Miguel, what is going on? It's almost dark; I don't have time for games."

"Helena, just give me and my cousin a ride back to Harford County please. Our car broke down back there, and the tow truck refuses to come to this neighborhood."

Helena was suspicious of Miguel's story but recognized his cousin Ernesto from the office as well. She unlocked the doors and allowed the two men to enter. She never noticed the third man jump in. As she drove off, she felt something cold on the back of her neck.

"Don't turn around. Just keep driving straight. I don't want to hurt you, but I will if I have to."

Helena's blood ran cold as she realized her coworkers had allowed her to be carjacked. She remembered every warning ever given on the Internet, by the media, and most of all her mother.

"Is this the chick with the rich boyfriend?" the unknown figure asked.

"Miguel says she's going to be worth millions. Her fiancé used to play for the Ravens. I'm sure we can get money."

"My fiancé doesn't have that money any more. But I have about $1,500 cash in the bank I can give you if you leave us alone."

The three men were silent as Helena drove toward Essex.

"What bank are you with?"

Helena pointed to the bank branch ahead. The men directed her to pull in and make a withdrawal so they can see the bank balance. Helena prayed Taurean didn't put the wedding cash into the joint account.

"Don't turn around. We don't want the cameras to show you were looking at someone else."

Helena slid the ATM card into the machine and entered her PIN number. She requested the maximum withdrawal of $300 and a receipt. The cash slid out of the machine, which Helena quickly grabbed. Helena pulled the receipt out of the slot and exhaled. The receipt showed a balance of $1,200. She walked back to her vehicle and handed the cash and receipt to the unknown gunman.

"You weren't lying to us. Drive down the street toward the next branch. We are going to make a few withdrawals tonight. If you cooperate we will let you go."

Three additional times the men got the cash and receipt. Shortly after midnight, the four pulled up to the final bank branch. Helena repeated the steps, grabbed the cash, receipt, and walked back to the car. She handed over the cash and receipt. Helena was prepared to be left on the side of the road as soon as the men got their hands on the last of the cash.

"You've been holding out! There's almost forty thousand in the account now," yelled the gunman.

"I thought she only had $1,500." Ernesto yelled as he nervously looked up and down the street.

Helena knew in her heart of hearts she would not be set free. The men heckled and yelled at her all the way to the drug den. They pulled her from house to house as they scored their powder heroin. Every few hours they rode to an ATM and made a withdrawal.

During a brief encounter with clarity, Miguel Fernandez had an "aha" moment.

"Let's take some of the money up to the casino in Perryville. I'm feeling lucky. Besides my cousin has finally perfected counting cards and thinks we can score big."

"Man, can you really count cards? I don't know about this. I'm not going back to jail," the third man said.

The three men made Helena drive up to Perryville to the casino. When they walked into the casino, there was a larger than life cutout of Taurean Harris with his fiancée holding the casino's chips.

"Forget counting cards. We've got Mrs. Harris. She can get us a line of credit so we can win big." The four-some walked over to the cashier. Helena gave them the ATM card and punched in the PIN number. The cashier approved a $30,000 cash advance.

The men moved around from the slots to the table games. Miguel was like a kid in a candy store. He threw down chips, and for a little while he won. Helena counted the chips on the poker table in front of him. There was over $50,000 in chips.

"Man, go ahead and cash out," Ernesto told his cousin.

"I've got this. I can win this last hand and make almost $100,000."

"Don't be stupid. Let's get the money and get out of here," Ernesto pleaded with his cousin.

Helena watched the horror unfold as the chips were scooped up by the dealer after Miguel lost the hand. The men had used all of the money she had in the account and were fronted $5,000 more because of Taurean's name. There was no way they had $5,000 between the four of them.

Security arrived to escort them to the Pit Boss, who didn't look too friendly. The men immediately started hemming and hawing. Helena tried to get the Pit Boss to take her away or call the police but to no avail. He realized she was the girl from the advertisement in the lobby.

"I don't want to embarrass your man, but you will need to get my money. I can give you a chance to call him."

Helena looked the guy square in the eyes and said, "My soon-to-be husband didn't approve that line of credit. These fools kidnapped me and forced me to come here. They stole from you and from me!"

The Pit Boss read Helena's eyes and decided she was truthful. The guy next to him tapped his ear and leaned over to the Pit Boss. A tall man with a wicked scar came into the room and walked behind Miguel.

"Well, look who we have here. It's the high roller from our other casino down on the shore. You are into us for $50,000 right now. Why should we front you another $5,000?"

Miguel turned quickly and almost fainted at the sight of the guy he called the "Enforcer." The guy was no joke and established a reputation for recovering money for the casino. Miguel looked at Ernesto and silently begged for forgiveness.

"Sir, can I speak to you in private?" Miguel motioned toward a corner of the room.

"We snatched Mrs. Harris late last night. Her man put $25,000 in her account at midnight. If he has $25,000 maybe he has millions. I bet Mrs. Harris here doesn't know all the money her man has. I think he'd be willing to spend a pretty penny to get her back."

The Enforcer grabbed Miguel by his collar and shook him for good measure.

"We don't get involved in things like this. It brings too much attention on our operations. It's idiots like you that are dangerous. You watch too much reality TV and get yourselves in trouble. Don't mix us in this garbage. You have three days to get my money."

Miguel shook his head, signaled Ernesto to leave, and grabbed Helena's hand.

"Miguel, what the hell were you saying over there? We are in too deep. I don't know about any of this." Ernesto shook his head and sighed deeply. "I can't believe I'm in the middle of gambling debts, drugs, and now a freaking kidnapping."

"Man, shut up. I'm trying to think of a way to get us out of this. We can't let her go, so we are going to take her with us. We are going to get the money for her and pay off the casino."

"Can't you ask Uncle Guillermo for the money?"

"I've been cut off. How many times do I have to tell you that, you idiot? I don't have anything to lose at this point. If we don't come up with the money that guy back there is going to kill me. If her guy doesn't give us the money, and I have to kill her, I will go to jail. Nothing to lose…"

Miguel and Ernesto quickly walked Helena back to the car. As they got ready to pull off, they spied a drunken guy walking toward a white van. He threw up and passed out on the side of the van. The two men grabbed the keys, threw Helena in the seat between them, and pulled out of the parking lot.

"Oh great, add auto theft to the charges," Ernesto smirked.

Helena began to cry in earnest over her fate. Miguel punched her hard enough to knock her out cold. The next thing she remembered was the dog barking outside of the van.

Helena looked around the room, which suddenly filled with activity. She was exhausted.

"When can I see my fiancé?" Helena asked the agent closest to her.

"I believe Mr. Blackman is working on the arrangements right now. Ma'am, you've been through a lot, and we appreciate all of the details you provided. We hope to use it to catch your kidnappers." The older gentleman gently cradled her hand in his as he escorted her toward the door.

"You two will be on a retreat for the next few days. I've packed some things for you two, and you'll be taken to Western Maryland while we handle some loose ends here. Ms. Green and another of my assistants will chaperone the retreat," Guy said.

Taurean shook his head in agreement. "This isn't the end of this is it?"

"No, I believe we have stumbled on to something much bigger than a kidnapping. You will be taken to one of my safe houses. Give me your telephone because it has GPS, which the kidnappers tracked. Our location is safe as is the whole industrial park. Here's a cell phone, which is pre-programmed with my number and Jax's number just in case."

"Guy, I don't know how to thank you for all of this?"

"Just invite me to your wedding."

They shook hands, and Guy made his way to his private office. While Helena was questioned, Ms. Green sent Guy a text message letting him know she escorted the detective to his office. Detective Betancourt had been kept waiting long enough.

"Detective, how are you doing?"

"I don't know how you get the information you have or how you are able to circumvent our laws, but your guys did a good job out there. I'm glad I listened to you and didn't jump all over the guy in the white t-shirt."

"My men are tracking him and the boater down. Not to worry, you and your team will get credit for this bust."

"I don't want credit— I want action." The detective smacked her fist into her palm.

"Detective, I will give you all the action your heart can stand," Guy said.

Detective Betancourt looked at Guy Blackman. He was tall, lean, and all male. But he wasn't Jax. She knew Jax couldn't stand her, but she had never been turned down by a man and she didn't like it.

"You don't have to pine after a man who doesn't want to be bothered with you. I'm standing right here and have been patiently waiting for you to get over your obsession. I'm not sure how much longer I can take it."

The detective shook her hair with her hand and looked at her feet. She knew she had to move past this thing with Jax. But Guy Blackman scared her. He was rich beyond imagination, had every resource available to mankind, and for some reason wanted her in the worst way.

She looked up at the bane of her existence and smiled softly.

"I'm not that easy. You will have to pursue me if you want me. I'm not going to fall all over you like you are probably used to. I'm my own woman, and I can stand on my own two feet. 'Ligeann a fhail reidh le tormain'," she called out over her shoulder as she left his office.

Guy laughed.

"Get ready to rumble indeed." He quickly translated her Irish comment as he watched her walk out the door.

Guy dialed the familiar numbers and waited for the call to connect.

"Jax, I just wanted to let you know we found Helena, and everyone is okay. I sent Taurean and Helena with a few of my security team members out to Western Maryland."

"Guy, I appreciate the call. I know your team is the reason for the safe return. I'm sure there is more to the story than you are letting on."

"The collaborative decided not to release the rescue to the media. As far as the kidnappers are concerned, she is still in the back of the van. The feds are waiting to locate all of the other players before making the announcement."

"I'll let Gertrude and Roxie know the good news but explain they need to keep it to themselves."

"By the way, I think I solved your stalker problem."

"Guy, you never give up do you? I hope she is worth all of your attention. I'm going to keep you in my prayers," Jax said. He laughed as he hung up.

Guy put his cell phone in his pocket as he turned his attention to the video surveillance from the rescue. He knew Brick and Mortar were reviewing the tapes in the hopes of spotting Gersaiim or one of his accomplices.

CHAPTER 13

The HR office was humming with activity. Rachel walked through the halls and wondered if her coworkers even cared about Helena's whereabouts or whether she was still alive.

Rachel could not believe the HR office was open on a Saturday. The Senior HR Officer called for mandatory overtime in order to prepare for the end of the fiscal year activity. The HR office processed retirements and new hire activities year-round, but the end of the fiscal year produced the most activity.

In order to accommodate the number of retirees requesting to process out of the system, HR was open today to receive the retirement packets. All hands were on deck to notarize, review forms, offer benefits information, and hold hands.

Rachel looked over at Miguel Fernandez and worried about his haggard look. He didn't appear to have slept at all in the last few days. He barked at customers and didn't seem as patient as he usually is during these events.

"Why don't you take these forms back over there and fill them out correctly?" Miguel said flatly to the waiting couple.

"Ma'am, let me see if I can be of assistance," Rachel said to the couple and accompanied them to the table. She pored over the forms and found the blank space. "Please put your initials in this box. That's it. You are all done." Rachel detached the couple's copies and folded them neatly into an envelope.

"Have a great weekend," Rachel called out as she walked over to Miguel. "You are out of control and in need of a shower." Rachel was astonished at Miguel's obvious lack of personal hygiene.

"Don't worry about me. I'm okay. I'll be fine." Miguel turned his back on his coworker.

Rachel grabbed Miguel under his arm and pulled him into the hallway away from prying eyes and ears.

"Just what the heck is going on with you, Miguel? This isn't like you."

"You think you know me. You haven't a clue of who I am. I'm sick of this place." Miguel walked away from Rachel and headed toward the men's room.

"If I didn't know any better I would swear he was high," Rachel murmured as she walked back into the large conference room.

"Excuse me miss, can you help me?"

Rachel headed over to the older gentleman near the window. She spent several minutes with the man assisting him and answering questions. She soon forgot about her missing in action coworker.

Miguel made his way down the rear staircase toward the Information Resources Management department break room. He spotted Justin over by the refrigerator.

"Hey man, I'm tapped out. Do you have anything for a headache?"

Justin reached in his pocket and pulled out a stamp sized plastic bag full of white powder. "Do you have my money?"

"I'm a little short right now. Here's fifteen dollars. I will get you the rest on my break. I'm in the middle of a benefits meeting."

Justin handed Miguel the bag and snatched the money out of his hand. "Don't forget me. If I'm short, we both are going to be in trouble."

Miguel raced up the stairs toward the men's room. As he rounded the last stairwell, a tall figure blocked his movement. Miguel looked up just as the fists rained down on his head knocking him back down the stairwell.

"I don't have the money on me," Miguel managed to choke out from his busted lips.

"When are you going to have it?" asked the shorter of the two.

"I should have it by five p.m., just like I told your boss."

"Well now we have to add interest so now you are into the boss for $60,000," said the other man as he added a kick to the groin for good measure.

Both men made their way out of the stairwell and departed the building from the side entrance. Miguel struggled up the stairs as he looked around for his missing bag. He spent ten minutes scouring the stairwell only to realize the men must have taken his drugs.

He walked out of the stairwell just as Detective Betancourt walked out of the women's restroom.

"I was just looking for you, Mr. Fernandez. Your coworker thought you had gone home, but I noticed your vehicle parked outside. What happened to you?"

Miguel fixed his good eye on the detective and stated, "I just fell down the steps. I'm a little sore, but I'll be okay."

"How about you take a ride with me over to the station? I have a few questions for you. I don't think you want your coworkers to overhear our conversation."

"If it's all the same to you, I'll decline your offer. I've got a lot of work to do, and I need to get back in the conference room."

Detective Betancourt looked at the bold young man standing in front of her and shook her head. As her gaze slipped downward, she spied a small plastic bag of white powder sticking out of his pant cuff. She reached down and fished them out.

The detective slapped a pair of handcuffs on Miguel and said, "Actually it wasn't a request. You are under arrest for possession of an uncontrolled substance." The detective read him his rights as she led him out to the waiting squad car.

Rachel saw all of the activity from the conference room door. She pulled out her cell phone and called Gertrude.

"Hi, you've reached Gertrude. Unfortunately, I'm on the phone...," Rachel disconnected without leaving a voice mail.

She watched as Miguel was seated in the back of the squad car. As their eyes connected, Rachel sent up a silent prayer for her coworker. Rachel turned back to the crowd of employees and began to assist with the paperwork.

Jax and Gertrude pulled up to the front of the building just as Detective Betancourt pulled off.

"I wonder what the Detective was doing here?" said Gertrude.

"I'm not sure, but I don't think it has anything to do with either one of us." He smiled at Gertrude as he thought of last night's lighthearted mood after the news of Helena's rescue settled in.

Gertrude, Jax, and Roxie watched a number of comedy movies and talked all night.

Jax showed the ladies to their guest rooms and headed off to his own. Gertrude called him back into her room and shut the door.

"Don't worry, Jax, I won't bite you," Gertrude whispered in his ear as she wrapped her long arms around his neck. Jax embraced Gertrude as she drew closer to him.

"Thank you so much for everything. I really look forward to getting to know you better."

"It's been a pleasure having the two of you here. This house has been quiet for far too long."

They kissed goodnight, and Jax walked out of the bedroom. He strode down the hall toward the other room and called out goodnight to Roxie.

The next morning Roxie announced she wanted to go to Teddy's house. Teddy, Roxie, and Jenna were planning to go out to eat breakfast. Jax, Gertrude, and Roxie piled into his truck. The trio rode over to Teddy's house in Joppa.

Roxie and Jenna screamed like fourteen-year-olds at the sight of one another. Gertrude walked over and gave both the girls hugs. She introduced Jenna and Jax to each other. Teddy and Jax stood off to the side while the women made small talk.

Jax and Gertrude said their goodbyes and headed for the truck. Jax reached for Gertrude's hand as they walked in companionable silence.

Jax made his way around the truck to open the passenger door for Gertrude. He helped her down and walked her to the building.

"There are a lot of people moving in and out of the building for a Saturday morning," Jax said as he held the door for a departing elderly couple.

"We are holding an end of the fiscal year retirement meeting. It's one of the most sought after events. We normally have to turn late registration folks away."

Gertrude and Jax walked into the conference room. Gertrude spotted Rachel finishing up with a customer. As the employee walked away, Gertrude walked up.

"Can you help me with this form?" Gertrude jokingly asked.

"Just a moment miss..." Rachel looked up at her girlfriend and screamed. "I called you a while ago. What's going on with Helena? Where's Jax? How is Jenna?"

"Calm down. Everything is everything. We can't talk about it openly, just know our prayers were answered. Jenna is doing fine. We just left Jenna, Teddy, and Roxie. The three were headed to breakfast."

"Well praise God. Are you here to help out? We could use your help."

Rachel turned and motioned to all of the customers waiting for assistance. Gertrude walked over to Jax and hugged him gently.

"I'm going to have to pitch in. I will call you later."

"Call me when you are ready to go, and I will come and get you."

"Jax, you have to work. You don't have time to chauffer me around. I can get Rachel to drop me at home."

"Don't worry about my job. I will be back for you. Besides Rachel looks like she needs to go home and rest." Jax kissed Gertrude on the lips and said goodbye to Rachel.

Gertrude took a good look at her girlfriend and realized Jax was right. "Rachel, did John drop you off?"

Rachel shook her head yes as she waddled off to the restroom. Gertrude pulled out her cell phone and called Rachel's husband.

"John, I think Rachel needs to go home. You may want to swing by the hospital because I think your wife may be going into labor."

"I'm on my way," John said. Gertrude hung up the phone and followed Rachel into the restroom.

"Rachel, honey, are you all right?" Gertrude searched the stalls for her friend.

"Gertrude, something isn't right. I wet my pants and I feel like I'm going to throw up."

"Rachel, everything is fine. You are going into labor. Your husband is on his way."

"I can't have this baby right now. We still have four weeks to go…" Rachel's speech was cut short by the pain hitting her abdomen.

"Remember to breathe, Rachel." Gertrude reached into the stall and helped her friend to her feet. The pair gingerly made their way to the employee entrance near the side door.

John had the car door open and looked tenderly at his wife. "Honey, it's going to be okay. I called the doctor, and she will meet us there. Thanks Gertrude, for taking care of my baby until I could get here."

Gertrude hugged John as he walked back toward the driver side. She watched as they drove toward Upper Chesapeake hospital.

Gertrude realized the pair left before they prayed, but she covered them with prayer as she made her way back toward the conference room. As much as Gertrude wanted to follow them, she did not. This was a family moment, and she would be an unwanted intrusion.

Gertrude attended to her customers and completed paperwork alongside her coworkers. After a few hours, the crowds thinned and the HR staff was able to take a much needed breather.

Gertrude headed to her office to get bottled water when she saw Chuck Tobias in his office. His head was laid on his desk. Gertrude tapped lightly on the desk, but Chuck didn't raise his head.

"Go away. I'm busy," Chuck's normally clear voice was slurred.

"I'm coming in any way, Chuck. What the heck is going on around here? I know you are not sitting in here drunk." Gertrude looked back down the hall to make sure no one was behind her.

"I'm not drunk; I'm sleepy."

Chuck struggled to keep his eyes open. Gertrude walked around to his side of the desk and took a good look at Chuck. She felt his pulse, which was normal.

"Chuck, have you been here all night?"

"I'm trying to finish screening all of the applications. If I don't I'm toast."

"What are you mumbling about?"

"The guy said if I don't get his last person hired I'm toast."

Gertrude realized Chuck was delirious and full of information.

"What guy?"

"We've got to get the last foreign worker hired before the July 1 deadline or else."

Gertrude tried to rouse Chuck to no avail. It was clear her coworker was sound asleep. He was too big for her to pull out of his chair, but he couldn't be seen with his head on the desk. Gertrude spun Chuck's chair around toward the window. She pushed him down in his chair, so you couldn't spot his head from the doorway. She eased out of the door and pulled out her cell phone.

"This is Jax."

"Hey babe, I just spoke to Chuck Tobias. He says he has to hire some foreign workers before July 1 or he is toast."

Jax disconnected the call and made a call to Guy. He passed along the information he received from Gertrude as well as the arrest of Miguel Fernandez.

Miguel was taken to the Sheriff's office. He waived his right to an attorney and provided all kinds of information to Detective Betancourt.

Gertrude wondered about the foreign workers Chuck spoke of hiring. She scrolled through her cell phone until she located the number of the person with answers.

"This is Kendra."

"Kendra, this is Gertrude. How are you doing?"

"I'm okay just a little sore and a little hungry."

"I'm glad you are okay. Tell Stan I said 'hi.'"

"How did you know Stan was here?"

"That man has been after you for years. If he had a chance to be in your presence I know he would take it."

"Well we are just friends."

"Friends are good to have. One day you and I are going to have a chat, but for now, I'm glad he's there with you. I called you to ask a question. Do you have a moment?"

"I'm waiting to be released so yes, I'm free."

"Chuck mentioned some foreign workers he had to hire. Were you recruiting foreign workers?"

"I wasn't recruiting any workers. Chuck was working with an agency to recruit security analysts from Europe. It was strange because I usually recruit all of the IT positions. I just figured Madeline wanted Chuck to handle it."

"Kendra, you've been most helpful. I'm going to call and check on you later on. If you need anything before I call you, please call me. I know you don't have any family, and I don't want you to feel all alone. I'm praying for your healing. Be well."

"Take care, Gertrude. Thanks for calling."

Gertrude hung up her phone and walked out of her office back to Chuck's office.

As she approached his office, she could hear Chuck on the phone.

"Sir, I'm telling you, we don't have another security analyst vacancy. I've placed the other two, but I just don't have a position for this last one."

Chuck's voice quieted as he listened to the caller on the other line. Gertrude peered through the door and noticed Chuck sweating profusely and his face reddening.

"You can just stop with all the threats. I've done more than enough for you guys. You can't get blood from a turnip. We don't have a vacancy, so you will have to try somewhere else!"

Chuck slammed down the phone and turned toward the door. When he spied Gertrude, he pulled out his handkerchief and wiped his forehead and face before speaking.

"What the heck are you looking at? Don't you respect a person's privacy?"

"Chuck, what is going on? Who are you being threatened by?"

"Don't worry about it. I was just joking with my friend on the other line. That's what happens when you snoop; you have a tendency to get the facts twisted." Chuck exhaled deeply as he walked past Gertrude and turned toward the front door.

Gertrude strode up beside Chuck and touched his arm gently.

"Chuck, if you need help just say so. Don't let your pride get you hurt. I know some people who can help you out of this mess."

"Gertrude, I appreciate your offer, but I've got it covered. It will all work out in the end. I'm going home, and I suggest you get out of here, too. Enjoy the rest of your weekend."

Gertrude shook her head as Chuck walked out of the suite. She walked back to Chuck's office. The door was cracked open, so she entered under the pretense of checking for burglars.

She walked around to his desk and rifled through his folders. Chuck's desk wasn't neat and orderly. He had piles of folders spread all over the office. Gertrude had nothing but time, so she methodically looked at the files and if it didn't catch her attention, she laid it aside.

Employers were hard-pressed to find degreed, certified, and experienced security analysts. Over the last few years, the agency increased the number of H1-B

Visa sponsorships of foreign workers. The employer would sponsor a foreign worker under the temporary program for a period of three years. The employer must pay the foreign workers the same wage as a U.S. Citizen.

Gertrude peered at all of the files laid out around Chuck's office. She didn't dare open his drawers to look for documents. She sat in his chair and looked around his office. Her eyes were drawn to the bookshelf in the corner. She saw a red folder wedged between two HR manuals. Gertrude walked over to the bookshelf and extracted the folder.

"Bingo! I knew that man was hiding something."

Chuck was in too deep. He was going to need some serious help. The folder contained information on the applicants, copies of the H1-B Visa petitions Chuck signed, and receipts showing non-refundable application fees of $5,000 each. There were over twenty-five applicants' information in the folder.

Gertrude quickly walked out of the office toward the copier. She made copies of all of the documents, placed them in the folder, and put the folder back where she found it. She pulled out her cell phone and left a message for Jax telling him she was ready to go.

She walked toward her office and noticed her door was ajar. She remembered closing the door. She turned to walk in the opposite direction when she felt a hand on her shoulder.

Gertrude screamed at the top of her lungs while thrusting her leg backward and connecting with the knee of the assailant.

"Gertrude, what is wrong with you? Why do you insist on attacking me?" Jax asked as he massaged his knee cap.

"Oh baby, I'm so sorry. My nerves are bad because of all the things going on in this office. It's crazy." Gertrude hugged Jax and kissed his pouted lips. "Forgive me?" she asked, while flashing a heart-melting smile.

"I forgive you and am thankful you do not carry a gun. You are a little too quick on the draw for me." Jax smiled as he escorted Gertrude out of the office suite.

"As long as I'm the only one quick on the draw." Gertrude winked at Jax, whose smile momentarily disappeared at the comment.

Jax burst out laughing and grabbed Gertrude around the waist as they made their way toward his truck. He opened the truck door and let her inside. Jax seated her and noticed the stack of papers she had in her hand.

"What do you have there?" he asked.

"Another piece of the puzzle. This case is getting stranger by the day."

"What case? Gertrude, you are not on a case. Leave this to the professionals."

"What is with you men— first Darius and now you. If I say I'm on a case, I'm on a case. I may not be licensed to carry a gun, but I occasionally assist the police in solving cases."

"What police have you assisted?" Jax asked.

"Columbo, Kojack, even that fine Laurence Fishburne who used to be on CSI."

"Just what I thought—another chair-side detective. Baby this is dangerous work. You are not a professional, and I don't want you to get hurt."

"I don't want to get hurt either. So I will take the folder with all of the documentation on the illegal activities back into the office where I found it. I will wait for the police to discover what I already know."

Gertrude took off her seatbelt and started to get out of the truck. Jax gently laid his hand on her thigh.

"Baby, I'm sorry. I offended you. You have been a big help to me on this case. Don't take the folder back. Let me see it."

"I will let you see it after you take me somewhere and feed me. I've been here all day and I need some nourishment."

"What do you feel like?"

"How about Famous Daves? I like their ribs and chicken."

"Famous Daves it is." Jax pulled the truck into traffic and headed toward the restaurant. "So tell me about this information you found."

"Well I stumbled across it while closing Chuck's door. What do you know about foreign worker programs?"

"Are you talking green cards?"

"Sort of. Green cards are permanent workers. When an employer wants to hire a temporary foreign worker they petition the U.S. Customs Immigration Service for an H-1B Visa. The employee is brought over for three years."

"That doesn't sound illegal."

"It's not illegal. What is illegal is for the employer to charge the employee a non-refundable 'application fee.' It seems Chuck was charging the employees $5,000 each. I found twenty-five petitions and receipts for fees.

Jax whistled as he pulled the truck into the parking lot. "That's a lot of money. Does the agency get the money?"

"The agency doesn't charge a fee, Jax.

"Chuck charged $5,000 fees to the employees. Why don't they tell anyone?"

"Most of the time they are scared to because they most likely borrowed money to get here and have no friends or family here. If they lose the H1-B, they have to return to their countries. The fees are not refunded to them."

"How many of the foreign workers do you normally hire?"

"In the last few years, maybe one or two. But it seems this year, Chuck intended to place at least twenty-five."

"You had twenty-five openings?"

"Not for security analysts. We only had two openings in the last year."

"So if you didn't have the security analyst jobs, where did they place the employees?"

"That's a good question. We've got to find out."

Jax opened Gertrude's door and helped her down from the truck. They walked toward the entrance to the restaurant.

"Welcome to Famous Daves. How many are in your party?"

Jax looked at Gertrude and back at the hostess. "Two please." The two followed the hostess to a cozy booth in the rear of the restaurant. They sat down and shortly thereafter a young waitress appeared to take their order. They gave their food and drink selections and settled into the booth. The food arrived after a few minutes. Jax said grace and they began to eat their food.

"Jax, I want to thank you for everything. I really appreciate you taking me and Roxie to your house."

"I'm glad I did, too. It seems your relationship with Roxie has changed."

"It did. I realized I mistreated the girl all of these years because I didn't trust her. I kept waiting for her to do something to Jenna. But I never really saw her for the young woman she was trying to be. I can't make it up to her, but I will treat her differently."

"I was shocked to hear she was living in her car. Not because she is young because there are thousands of homeless her age. I was shocked because she was your daughter's best friend."

Jax looked at Gertrude and took her hand. "I'm a third party looking at this thing with fresh eyes and you were rough on the girl. I know you didn't know she was homeless, but it seemed you didn't care for her."

Gertrude's eyes watered as she felt the conviction of Jax's words. She knew in her heart she hadn't treated the young lady like her second daughter. In fact, she treated her worse than a stranger.

Jax offered Gertrude a napkin as he continued talking. "I know you were protecting your daughter and doing what you felt was best. As a Christian you know we are called to treat people kind even those who we feel do not have our best interest in mind. I believe you are a warm and wonderful woman."

Gertrude looked up from her plate and watched Jax's facial expression change from serious to inviting as he smiled at her gently.

"It's okay, Jax. You haven't said anything to me that I didn't say to myself last night. I replayed all of the years and things I've said to that girl and wanted to die. I was often cruel for no reason. The thing is, she and I are more alike than Jenna and me. But she's a good kid in spite of her horrible childhood."

"Well we just will have to make certain we love on her every chance we get."

"I like how you keep saying 'we' as if there is a 'we'," Gertrude laughed.

"We are a 'we' and there is no going back." Jax placed cash on top of the check and reached for Gertrude's hand. He pulled her to her feet and walked them out of the restaurant.

Gertrude's cell phone started to chime with her play sister's ring tone.

"What's up Nenie?" Gertrude said to her best friend Jenine who was more like a sister. The two had been friends through two marriages and divorces. Jenine had recently married William, a wonderful man who treated her like a queen. The couple lived in another state a few hours south of Gertrude.

"Girl, I've been calling you the last few hours in between clients. What's up with you?"

"Chick, there is so much drama we don't have enough time right now. I just left the restaurant with my friend Jax and we are on our way to his truck."

"Jax…uh huh… When did we meet this man? What does he do?"

"Nenie, I'm going to have to call you back later. We will chat. Kiss my niece for me, and tell my brother-in-law I said 'hi.'"

"Rushing me off the phone for a man? This is serious. Call me tonight. Smooches."

"Smooches." Gertrude hung up the phone and turned her attention back to Jax.

"You didn't have to rush your friend off of the phone."

"Yes I did. I wanted to continue our conversation and it would be rude of me to do otherwise. I would want your full attention."

"Good because I aim to give you my full attention when I get you back to my house."

Jax steeled his gaze on Gertrude as he opened the truck door. Gertrude slid past Jax and climbed into the truck. He bent his head and stole a kiss before closing the door. He quickly walked around to the driver's side and entered the truck.

The pair rode in silence toward Jarrettsville. Jax pulled the truck into his driveway a few minutes later. He walked around the truck and helped Gertrude out. A few bunnies hopped around the front yard while a deer slipped through the trees a few feet away.

"You've got a wildlife preserve here." Gertrude remarked as they walked toward the front door.

Jax entered the foyer and disarmed the alarm system. Jax reached for Gertrude as soon as the front door closed. He pulled her in an embrace and nuzzled her neck.

"What is that scent? It's been driving me crazy all day."

"I usually wear Tom Ford Black Orchid, but today all I had was some generic body wash in my purse. I didn't scrounge around in your bathroom for anything else."

"I actually like the body wash on you. It's more feminine and flirty than the other fragrance."

Gertrude looked up into Jax's face. "Are you saying I smelled like a man this whole time?"

"No baby, what I'm saying is I prefer this fragrance. But since you ask, the Tom Ford is a little heavy for springtime."

Jax's cell phone rang. Gertrude had a lot to say but instead she fried him with her stares and walked toward the kitchen. Jax was close behind and opened the refrigerator door for her. Gertrude reached in, grabbed a bottle of water, and let herself out on the patio.

"Jax, this is Guy. I've been doing some checking. What do you know about foreign worker programs?"

"You are the second person to ask me that today. Gertrude said she found something in one of her coworker's office about the H-1B Visas."

"Originally I thought Gerasiim was here running a casino for the Russian mob. Turns out I'm partially correct. He's here for the mob, but they are running a foreign worker scheme. Seems they have connections within local agencies who petition the United States Citizenship and Immigration Services (USCIS) foreign workers with special skills. However, more than half of the workers end up on chicken farms or picking crabs as seasonal workers."

"Gertrude, come on in and talk to Guy," Jax called out as he held the cell phone out to Gertrude.

Gertrude snatched the phone out of Jax's hand.

Jax watched Gertrude pace the length of the patio while talking to Guy. Her face displayed a range of emotions; anger, disbelief, sadness, and finally pleasure. She glowed with emotion. Jax felt a sharp pain in his chest that he never felt before. He was jealous. The thought of Gertrude glowing over the attention of some other man didn't sit well in his spirit.

He opened the patio door and strode toward Gertrude. She had her back turned to him as she spoke to Guy.

"I really appreciate all that you've done for us. I don't know you; yet you've managed to rescue my coworker, gift two people I know with millions of dollars, and now you've figured out what's going on at HR. You are a man of many talents. I look forward to getting to know you better as well."

Gertrude turned toward Jax and handed him his cell phone. She walked over to the outdoor king-sized bed and lay down. Jax's eyes trailed behind her but gave her the privacy she obviously sought.

"What's up, Guy," Jax said gruffly.

"Man, what's up with you? You insult the woman and then want to take it out on me."

"I didn't insult her. She asked me a question and I was honest. What's wrong with that?" Jax asked incredulously.

"As gifted as you are musically, you are an idiot when it comes to women. You could have said something like 'I liked the other fragrance, but I prefer this body wash on you, it smells delightful' or something else along those lines."

"I was honest, and she didn't like it."

"You were unnecessarily cruel, and it hurt her. I would suggest you go fix it, Jax. Remember this woman isn't one of your perpetrators. She's a woman with feelings, and she trusts you with her heart. Don't keep stomping on it, Jax, or you will lose her." Guy gently prodded.

Jax shook his head as he realized his mistakes. He was cruel to Gertrude, and he suspected his friend's motives toward Gertrude.

"Jax, it's okay to be jealous. It shows you really care about her."

"How do you do that? It's like you read minds or something. I'm going to have to call you back. I've got some crow to eat."

"Just remember— the goal is to keep her happy, so you can be happy. Call me later." Guy disconnected the call.

Jax looked around the patio and spied a bush of purple hydrangeas in a corner. Farther down the walkway were some lilacs. Jax bent down, pulled out his pocket knife and cut a few flowers. He walked over toward the grill and retrieved a few twist ties from the overhead shelving.

Gertrude was lying on the bed gently snoring when Jax arrived. He lied down next to her and placed his arm holding the bouquet around her waist. The wonderful fragrance woke Gertrude and she smiled when she saw the bouquet.

"Thank you. It's lovely, Jax."

"Gertrude, I'm sorry for hurting your feelings. I shouldn't have said it."

"Jax, I overreacted. It's just that I couldn't always afford designer perfumes. One year Darius bought me the perfume for my birthday, and I've worn it ever since. The truth is, at first I thought it was a little heavy for me, too, but I've gotten accustomed to wearing it.

"The thing is, it was the last reminder of my ex-husband. I should have gotten rid of it years ago but couldn't. When you made the comment, it was like you were forcing me to choose between you and my ex. I've said I was over him, but I held on to this for so long. Is that sick or what?"

"There is nothing wrong with wearing it if it brings you pleasure. Have you ever thought wearing it may have continuously reminded you of darker days? Why keep yourself in bondage? You obviously can afford designer perfumes now, why not get a new fragrance? I'm not suggesting you change for me but for you. I adore you no matter what you smell like."

Gertrude turned over toward Jax and lifted her face in anticipation of Jax's kisses. The two enjoyed a few moments of affection until the front door chimed.

"I never get visitors out here. I wonder who that is."

Jax pulled Gertrude to her feet and handed her the bouquet. They walked to the front door. Jax opened the door and revealed a group of familiar faces.

Roxie, Jenna, Teddy, Guy, Brick, and Mortar.

"What a surprise. Looks like the gangs all here. Come in."

Jax moved away from the door and everyone walked to the kitchen. Jax closed the door but a dainty shoe prevented closure.

"Detective, what are you doing here?" Jax asked.

"I called her and told her to meet me here. I hope you don't mind." Guy walked toward the detective. He gently took her hand, kissed the back of it, and placed it in the crook of his arm.

"Come with me, so I can introduce you to everyone," Guy said.

Jax shook his head, peered out the front door for other guests, and shut the door. A lively discussion was going on as he walked into the kitchen.

He looked around and smiled at the sight. Roxie and the twins were off on one side of the kitchen discussing the kidnapping and rescue as they scarfed down what appeared to be leftovers from breakfast.

Detective Betancourt and Guy huddled over the breakfast nook in their own world. Gertrude talked to Teddy and Jenna in front of the refrigerator.

Jax thought, *this is the second time I have had company in my house*. Jax was always a loner. He didn't trust people enough to let them in his personal space.

He looked around and realized he missed the interaction and connection to others. He walked over to the refrigerator and grabbed a bottle of Barq's.

Gertrude finished up her conversation and looked at Jax. She walked to him and gently kissed him.

"Hey honey, what are you thinking?"

"I was just thinking this is the second time I've had guests at the house. That's what has been missing in here. I tried to fill it with music and other things."

She hugged him and turned to the group.

"You all are cutting into my alone time. Why are you here?" Gertrude said to the group.

"Looks like we showed up just in time I would say," Roxie yelled. "I told you both I take my chaperone duties seriously."

"I'm here unofficially at the invitation of one Guy Blackman," the detective said. "I do appreciate you letting me in your house, Jax. Gertrude, I owe you an apology. I was acting catty over someone who didn't know I existed."

Gertrude extended her hand and Detective Betancourt shook it. Jax and Guy walked over and claimed their respective women. Guy looked at the group and motioned them out to the patio. The group walked out and gathered around the large table set up in front of the grill area.

"I called everyone here so we can trade notes, brainstorm, and get to the crux of what is going on."

"I'm here unofficially, so please call me Erin," the detective informed the group. "I can't share official business, but I can answer general questions."

Gertrude stood up from the table and walked into the kitchen. She came back on the patio with a red folder, which she handed to Jax. He scanned it and handed it to Guy. He and Erin were reviewing the information when Guy's phone rang.

"This is Guy. William, what do you have for me?" Guy excused himself from the group and spent the next several minutes with the caller.

Gertrude leaned over to Erin. "So, are you two an item?"

"We haven't gotten that far but the chase is on, and I'm going to enjoy it. Looks like you and Jax are tight. I'm glad for you. He's a great guy." Erin grinned broadly.

"This is a little weird for me and uncomfortable. A few days ago you were out to take me down and now we are chatting like old pals," Gertrude said.

"Well we can be grown-ups or catty little girls. Our men are best friends, so we may as well kiss and make up, don't you think?"

Gertrude smiled and shook her head. "You are right. We can play nice in each other's sand box. Just remember— I don't like to share my man."

"Well good, because I don't plan to let you have my sloppy seconds either."

They laughed as the warnings were given and accepted. They talked about Jax's house, the beautiful patio and backyard.

"I'm sorry about the interruption. We have some new information that may shed light on what's going on," Guy said.

"Is anyone hungry or thirsty? Why don't we get something to eat and drink because this may take a while." Jax stood and walked toward the patio door.

"Jax, I've already taken care of it. If you will open the front door, my catering staff is dropping off enough food and drink to last a while. I've asked them to set up out here, since it's so nice," Guy said.

Jax and Gertrude walked to the front door and opened it for the catering staff. The staff walked in with buffet tables, chafing dishes, dinnerware, and desserts. Jax watched in amazement as the staff created an appetizing buffetscape with all sorts of meat, vegetables, salads, bread, and hot and cold items.

The group gathered around the buffet table and held hands. Jax said grace over the food, thanked God for friends—both old and new—and said amen. The group fixed their plates, poured drinks, and sat around the table. After a few minutes of silent dining, the group began to talk all at once. Snippets of conversations ranged from the kidnapping to the assault, to Jax's house, and back to the kidnapping.

Guy looked over the folders as he sent text messages to his people. Every few minutes he would look over at Erin and smile.

When they finished eating they cleaned off the tables; the caterers broke down the tables, boxed up the leftovers, and filled Jax's refrigerator and pantry. The small staff loaded up their van and pulled away from the property.

As they settled down, Guy started to speak. "It seems we are in the middle of an illegal operation, which involves several HR employees. The foreign workers scam is headed up by the eastern shore Russian mob contingent."

Gertrude spoke up. "I don't understand how our HR office got involved."

"My staff investigated the backgrounds of the employees in your office including Madeline Shaw, Worrell Stevens, Miguel Fernandez, Ernesto Santos, Sonya Kennedy, Denise Krapel, Rachel Ward, Chuck Tobias, Stan Winters, Justin Pickelford, Taurean Harris, Helena Perkins, and Kendra Walker."

Jax looked at Guy and he nodded unperceptively to indicate Gertrude checked out.

Guy continued, "we found some very interesting things out about your coworkers. It seems there are several involved in this scam. Miguel, Ernesto, Chuck, Justin, and Sonya have all played a part. Miguel, Ernesto, and Justin are also involved in the kidnapping of Helena Perkins.

"An unnamed source has determined that Chuck has been involved in making petitions to USCIS for years. He would provide the names to his contacts that would pay him well for his assistance. The contacts would then have their 'employees' apply for visas in the names Chuck provided. The employees would borrow from Russian money men and in exchange would redeem their kinsmen from the previous trips to the states."

Jax looked at Guy in amazement over the information. "So you are saying that someone's son would work here under a visa and when it expired, his cousin or someone back home would have to pay to bring him back, then exchange places and work in his stead?"

"That's right—only it gets deeper. The family member couldn't pay for both trips but would be forced to borrow even more money from the group. In essence they were indentured servants when they arrived stateside. There isn't any pay per se. They get some subsistence and are provided rooms, which they share with others in their situations."

The group sobered at the thought of the human trafficking going on right in their midst. They prayed for those caught in the vicious cycle. They also prayed for the safe return of the family members and for justice for the perpetrators.

"I remember Chuck telling us these fantastical stories of his travels around the world. When we would ask him how he got his money, he would say he won a lawsuit against a former employer," Gertrude said.

"Chuck wasn't telling a tale. He actually did settle with his former employer for almost five million dollars. He blew through his settlement within three years. He was borrowing money from a 'banker' to get through the tough times before he started working with your agency. When he was hired here, he was forced to begin making petitions for the group. He started off small with a few a petitions a year. But this year, he caught the eye of USCIS because he made over twenty-five petitions in the first half of the year," Guy said.

"Hey Boss, remember the guy in the white shirt at the ransom drop off?" Brick yelled to Guy. "He's Justin Pickelford. We were able to ID him from the HR photos. The other guy who jumped on the boat was Ernesto Santos."

"Guy, I will need copies of those photos so I can get warrants on them," Detective Betancourt said.

"Already took care of. I sent them over to the station anonymously." Guy kissed Erin.

"It's my turn." Erin stood and pulled a notebook out of her back pocket. "I have some information on Madeline Shaw and Worrell Stevens."

Gertrude turned her chair and took a sip of her iced tea.

"We questioned both Mr. Stevens and Ms. Shaw. As far as we can tell their assaults didn't have anything to do with the Perkins kidnapping. Unfortunately, we haven't confirmed their stories but are still investigating."

Detective Betancourt thought she heard everything in her line of work. It wasn't often she was caught off guard.

"Tell me again from the top. I believe I missed something," she said.

Worrell Stevens wished he could blink and this whole thing would go away.

"As I said, I walked in the office and saw Madeline with some sort of long rubber tubing or rope around her neck. It was wrapped around her ankles."

"Was there anyone else in the room? Was the office neat or was it tossed?"

"I didn't have a chance to get a good look. I got conked on the head right after I walked in."

The detective jotted notes in her pad and eyed Worrell. "Well was she happy, sad, surprised, or mad? Think, this is an important piece of information!"

"Now that I think about it, she had tears in her eyes and her makeup was running down her face."

"Close your eyes and try to imagine the scene again. Do you see anything out of the ordinary?"

"Her iPad is kind of propped up and facing her. That's it," Worrell said.

"How close are you and Ms. Shaw? My notes say you're married."

"I don't like what you're implying. I love my wife and would never do anything to jeopardize our relationship."

The detective slid her chair closer to the side of the bed. "I'm not implying anything. I'm trying to determine the nature of your relationship with Ms. Shaw."

"We are coworkers and nothing more. I love my wife." Worrell's face reddened and his lips were tight against his teeth.

"I don't mean to upset you. Is this the first time you've seen Ms. Shaw in a compromising position?"

"I don't understand?" Worrell said. "This is the first time I've worked late so I wouldn't know what she does in her office."

"Are there any rumors about Ms. Shaw's evening activities?"

"I don't listen to gossip and rarely associate with my coworkers. I'm friendly but I maintain my distance."

"If you think of anything else, you have my card." The detective stood and was on her way to the door when Worrell stopped her.

"Is she okay?"

"I'm on my way to check on her now. I can tell her you asked about her." The detective hesitated at the door and turned back to face Worrell.

"Is there anything else you want to tell me before I go speak to Ms. Shaw?" The detective fixed her gaze on Worrell and watched his expressions closely.

He averted his gaze and turned to face the wall. "No, nothing at all, detective."

Detective Betancourt walked out the door and headed toward the stairs. She jogged down the one flight and was almost to Ms. Shaw's room when she realized something. *Son of a gun, he never did answer my question.*

Detective Betancourt lightly knocked on Ms. Shaw's door.

"Come in," said Ms. Shaw.

The detective held out her hand to Ms. Shaw and introduced herself. "I'm Detective Betancourt and I'm here to ask you a few questions."

Madeline lowered her gaze as tears wet her cheeks and her chest heaved with sobs.

The detective looked around the room and walked over to the side table to get the box of tissues. She pulled a few from the box and handed them to Ms. Shaw.

"If you need a moment, I can come back if you like." Although the detective made an offer to leave she continued to sit in her chair.

Madeline wiped her face, blew her nose and balled the tissue up in her good hand.

"I'll tell you everything. You don't have to ask me questions."

The detective uncapped her pen and prepared to take notes.

"I know you've probably talked to Worrell and he told you what he saw. I want to explain."

The detective nodded slightly as she waited for her to continue. She sat up straight in the chair and leaned forward slightly in order to make certain she captured every detail.

"My husband and I play games. He's not dangerous, he's dying and bored. He spends all of his time on the internet trying to find different things to try before he dies. Unfortunately for me, I have to play along."

"I'm sorry to hear that."

"Don't be sorry. It'll all work out in the end. You're probably wondering about the ropes. My husband gave them to me so I could tie myself up. I video chat with him from my office and all is right in my world when I get home."

Detective Betancourt stood up and paced the room. "If you were tied up how did you get so seriously hurt?"

Madeline looked the detective in the face and smiled. "This whole thing is a comedy of errors. If you take a seat you'll see."

The detective sat down and stretched her legs in front of her. "I find that hard to believe but please, go on."

"Worrell Stevens is a nice man and he loves his wife tremendously. I fell in love with him shortly after

I hired him. He seemed like the kind of guy every mother hopes her daughter ends up with."

Madeline's face brightened as she talked about Worrell. "He was never out of line with me. Friendly but nothing that could be taken the wrong way. He's just a very nice guy. If he knew I was in love with him, he would probably talk me out of it or pray for me. He's just that kind of guy."

"Well last night, Worrell stopped by my desk on his way to Pat's Pizzeria."

The detective looked up from her notes. "About what time was that?"

"It must have been around ten thirty. I thought he was heading out to go home but he said he needed to pick up something to eat. He asked if I needed anything and I told him I really would like some waffle fries."

"What time did he get back?"

"He dropped off my fries around eleven o'clock. He said he was going back to his office to clean up and then head out for home. I was getting ready to er…video chat so I was waiting to hear him walk by. I thought I heard him walk out when I started. The next thing I know Amber Gray shows up."

"Who's Amber Gray?"

"She's a former employee that we let go. She had some sort of mental illness and was fine as long as she was medicated. When she wasn't medicated she became belligerent, physical, and threatened her supervisors. We tried to accommodate her but after a while she wasn't able to do the job and we had to remove her."

Madeline had just tied the last knot and was speaking softly into her iPad. She could see her husband's head roll back which indicated he was almost asleep. Just as she turned her computer off, the door opened.

"Well hello Ms. Shaw," the womanly voice called out.

Madeline turned quickly and cried out as the first punch hit her jaw.

"You remember me don't you? Amber Gray's my name. You fired me and ruined my life."

When Madeline saw the wide open stare, the spittle on the edges of her lips, and felt the hot breath on her face, she knew she would die.

The cord tightened around Madeline's throat and she prayed she would pass out before Amber killed her.

"I was over in the restaurant up the street. I was in the mood for a little fun and I spoke to a nice looking guy. He said he'd stay and chat but he had a boss that made him work late. I followed him from the restaurant. You messed up my chance to be with that nice man. You don't care about nobody and nothing but yourself." Each sentence was punctuated with a rock solid punch to her body. "Well look at you all tied up. What the heck is going on?"

Amber kicked Madeline out of the chair and dragged her around the office until she stopped moving. She picked her up and put her back in the chair. She walked around the desk to take a look at her handiwork. Amber reached down into her sweat pants and pulled out a long Jim Bowie serrated knife. She turned just as the door swung open trapping her behind it.

Worrell walked in the office. Madeline opened her tear filled eyes just in time to see Amber stab him. He hit his head on the desk as he fell forward.

"Amber ran towards the front door. I passed out from the pain right after that. I wonder how she got in the building," Madeline said.

Detective Betancourt stood up and walked out the front door. She quickly dialed the station and updated Detective Gentry on the latest information.

She walked back into the room and stood next to the bed. "You've had a rough time of it."

"Thank you but I'll be okay. I think of this as my penance for living a wild life a long time ago. I've made some very bad decisions and done some not-so-nice things. Besides, my husband has no one else and if this is what it takes to ease him into eternity, I'm willing."

"Well you take care. Oh, I almost forgot. Mr. Stevens asked about you."

"Is he okay? I hope he wasn't too seriously injured."

"I can tell you he is recovering."

"Thank you detective. I hope you find Amber before she hurts someone else."

"My men will get right on it."

The detective walked out of the room and decided to take the elevator to the first floor. She needed a moment to think about the info Ms. Shaw shared.

Detective Betancourt looked at the group. We were able to determine the blood on the door belonged to one Amber Gray, former employee. The knife in Jenna's tire was also hers."

"Amber Gray?" Gertrude shot to her feet. "I cannot believe that woman is still loose on the streets after the way she beat a coworker a few years back. What does she have to do with this?"

"It appears Ms. Gray may be responsible for Ms. Shaw's and Mr. Stevens' injuries. Ms. Gray walked out the front door right before Jenna pulled up to the office. From what we can tell she must have stabbed the tire to keep Jenna from driving away. She hit her in the head and ran away. We're still trying to determine how she got in the building."

Amber woke up with a bad taste in her mouth. She didn't know where she was or what time it was. She tried to gather her bearings and realized she was back in her room at the boarding house.

As she sat up in bed scenes from the previous night flashed in her mind. She couldn't put it all together but she smiled at the sight of Ms. Shaw's bloody body in the chair. *She deserved what she got. I was so close to bringing that man back to my place for some fun and she ruined it.*

Amber saw herself run out the front door but she grabbed the door before it slammed shut. She didn't remember seeing the car parked in front of the building. Before she knew it she stabbed the tire. *Now let's see that broad go home. I may need to come back and finish her off.* Amber heard movement from the front of the building and ran around the driver's side and knelt down. A young girl was coming towards the car and talking real fast on the phone. Amber grabbed the girl and slammed her head into the pole and ran towards the parking garage.

Amber rubbed her head and tried to think of good things, like her doctor told her in one of her sessions.

She worked at Nesbit Industries for most of her adult life. She was a good custodian. She especially loved mopping and buffing the floors. There was something beautiful about the movement back and forth across the floor. It was almost like dancing.

She was in a car accident which kept her in the hospital for almost three months. When she got out she would have these seizures that would send sharp pains across her skull. It seemed the only thing that made her feel better was hitting or breaking something. At first she broke pencils she found on the desks or broke up old pallets on the loading docks.

Pretty soon it didn't ease the pain. One smart mouth young janitor everyone called Dinky got on her bad side.

"You a big chick. I thought you was a dude for the longest time." Dinky said and laughed to the group standing in the break room.

A sudden flash of pain struck Amber and she felt like she passed out. When she came to they were loading Dinky in an ambulance. She was sitting in the supervisor's office.

"Ms. Gray, what can you tell me about the incident which occurred between you and Mr. James "Dinky"

Johnson?" Ms. Shaw from HR was sitting in a chair across from her with her legs crossed.

"He called me out my name and then I got a real bad headache. I don't remember nothing."

"You don't remember hitting Mr. Johnson in the face with your fist?"

"I just told you I don't remember." Amber tried to stand to her feet but became unsteady and stayed seated.

"We have five witnesses who reported you punched Mr. Johnson. Unfortunately, this kind of behavior is unacceptable. I'm afraid we have no choice but to suspend you for two weeks." Ms. Shaw handed her a letter and pointed to the line for Amber to sign her name.

"Well I'm sorry but I don't remember it. I'll be in on Monday on time."

"Suspension means you do not come to work and you do not get paid for two weeks. I'm sorry." Ms. Shaw stood up and closed her briefcase.

Amber grabbed her jacket. She hung her head and walked out of the building.

There were a few more instances of Amber blacking out over a period of three months. After the last incident she was called to the administration building. She was escorted into the HR conference room. She looked across the table and saw Ms. Shaw. A union rep walked in behind Amber and took a seat next to her.

Ms. Shaw handed Amber a letter. "This is the decision letter from the director. He is upholding your removal from your position as a custodian with Nesbit Industries effective immediately."

Amber couldn't believe that witch had the nerve to smile as she said it.

A sudden brilliant light sent a bolt of pain through Amber's skull. She rocked back and forth in the bed and howled until the pain caused her to pass out…

Gertrude shook her head in disbelief. "I'm just glad everyone is okay. If that woman had hurt my child…Help me Lord. I'm telling you all some good stuff. Working in HR all these years and these stories become more commonplace. I can't make this stuff up! This is crazy."

Jax walked over and rubbed Gertrude's back. He wrapped his arms around her and held her tightly to him.

The detective closed her notebook and put it back in her pocket. Guy walked over, took her hand, and placed a light kiss on the palm. He bent his frame to look her in the eye. "Are you okay?"

"I'll be fine. We've got our hands full but we'll get to the bottom of this."

"I know you can handle the work. I meant personally." Guy gently smiled at the detective.

"Stop looking at me like that. I'm good." The detective flashed her pearly whites at Guy and rubbed his arm.

"Roxie, did you want to come over and hang out with me and Teddy?" Jenna asked.

"No, I'm going to hang with Brick and Mortar. They've got some things back at the bat cave they want to show me. We'll hook up later." Roxie hugged Jenna and Teddy.

"Mom, we're going to go back to Teddy's place for a while. We are going to take his mom some food, and then I'm going back to my place."

"Jenna, I forgot to tell you I paid your rent for the next six months. I hope you don't mind." Roxie kissed Jenna and ran out the door behind Brick and Mortar.

"Wow, I cannot believe that girl. I'm so happy for her," Jenna said.

"I'm happy for you, too. You and Teddy look like you've made up for lost time."

"We are taking things slow and just hanging out for now. I'm more interested in what's going on with you and Jax. You seem very happy. I hope you are."

"I am happy. Jax treats me very well, and we are getting to know each other."

"Well you deserve to be happy. I'm just glad you've gotten over Daddy. I love my Dad, but you need to be loved the way you need to be loved."

"Thank you for your wisdom, daughter of mine. I love you and thank God you are okay. I'm also glad Roxie was okay. We had a long talk, and I apologized for the way I treated her all these years."

"Roxie wouldn't give me the details. She just said you guys worked it out, and we are all family again."

A cell phone rang, and everyone looked up as Jenna answered the call.

"Yes, this is Jenna Judkins. I am available on Monday for an interview. Yes, eleven o'clock will be fine. I look forward to meeting you soon."

Jenna disconnected the call and began to scream and pump her fists in the air.

"I have an interview on Monday for the Public Information Specialist position. They say I'm one of two people interviewing for the position."

"Oh baby, I'm so proud of you. I knew you were going to get the job."

"Mom, I'm just interviewing. Besides how do you know I got the job?"

"God didn't say application denied. I believe you walk in His favor. So you can claim that job. I love you sweetie," Gertrude said.

The group offered congratulations to Jenna, who basked in the good feelings shared by everyone.

Gertrude hugged Jenna and Teddy. The trio walked toward the door with the rest of the group as they parted company.

Guy and Erin walked with their arms around each other toward the front door. Erin stood on her tiptoes but only reached Guy's chest. He bent down, lifted her off her feet, and kissed her properly. He gently placed her back on the ground. They walked out to her vehicle, and he seated her inside the car.

"Call me when you get home."

"I've got to make a stop at the station first."

"Erin, be careful. We've contacted several government agencies, but you know how this can turn ugly before it's stopped," Guy said as he leaned into the door.

Erin stroked his face before planting a wet sloppy kiss on his lips. "*Beidh me glaoch ort.*" Erin closed the door and started the engine.

"You better call me or I will hunt you down, Detective Betancourt," Guy called out as he turned toward Jax and Gertrude.

"You take care of my partner, and remember what we talked about earlier. Have some patience with Jax. He will be worth it." Guy hugged Gertrude and turned toward Jax.

"I see you fixed it."

"You daggone right I fixed it. I saw that woman's tears and wanted to cut my tongue out. I'm getting ready to go in here and get on her good side. As always it's been something hanging out with you," Jax said.

"Well I'm glad we've had a chance to work together on this. Be careful because you know this is going to get ugly."

They shook hands, and Guy headed toward the waiting limousine. Jax watched the vehicle pull off and walked back into the house. He armed the alarm system and searched the house for Gertrude. He smiled as he noticed her lying on the outside bed.

"You do know there is a bed inside the house right?"

"If we go in that house, I may do things to you I will have to repent for later. I'm not so bold out here."

Jax laughed as they laid side by side under the setting sun. The two chatted and laughed as they shared intimate secrets under the watchful eyes of their Creator.

11/30/13

To Eunice

AGAINST COMPANY POLICY

Keep reading & living life out loud!

AGAINST COMPANY POLICY

HATTYE C. KNIGHT, PHR

Published by Tate Publishing & Enterprises, LLC
127 E. Trade Center Terrace | Mustang, Oklahoma 73064 USA
1.888.361.9473 | www.tatepublishing.com

Tate Publishing is committed to excellence in the publishing industry. The company reflects the philosophy established by the founders, based on Psalm 68:11,
"The Lord gave the word and great was the company of those who published it."

Cover design by Brandon Land
Interior design by Blake Brasor

Published in the United States of America

ISBN: 978-1-62024-443-2
1. Fiction, Suspense
2. Fiction, Crime
12.06.15